Also by Barry Hannah

Captain Maximus

CAPTAIN

MAXIMUS

stories by

BARRY

HANNAH

Alfred A. Knopf

New York 1985

*The author expresses his deepest thanks
to the John Simon Guggenheim Memorial Foundation
for its support in the writing of this book.*

THIS IS A BORZOI BOOK
PUBLISHED BY ALFRED A. KNOPF, INC.

"Fans" originally appeared in *Atlanta Weekly*. "Ride, Fly,
Penetrate, Loiter" originally appeared in *The Georgia Re-
view*. "Even Greenland" was originally published in a chap-
book by Barry Hannah in 1983. "Power and Light" originally
appeared in a limited edition published by Palaemon Press.
Copyright © 1983 by Barry Hannah and Stuart Wright. "It
Spoke of Exactly the Things" originally appeared as "Black
Butterfly" in a limited edition published by Palaemon Press.
Copyright © 1982 by Barry Hannah and Stuart Wright. "I
Am Shaking to Death" originally appeared in *Quarterly
West*.

Library of Congress Cataloging in Publication Data
Hannah, Barry.
Captain Maximus.
I. Title.
PS3558.A476C3   1985   813'.54   84-48738
ISBN 0-394-54458-7

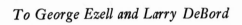

To George Ezell and Larry DeBord

Contents

Captain Maximus

Getting Ready

He was forty-eight, a fisherman, and he had never caught a significant fish. He had spent a fortune, enough for two men and wives, and he had been everywhere after the big one, the lunker, the fish bigger than he was. His name was Roger Laird, better off than his brother, who went by the nickname "Poot."

Everywhere. Acapulco, Australia, Hawaii, the Keys. Others caught them yesterday and the weather was bad today and they were out of the right bait. Besides, the captain was sick and the first mate was some little jerk in a Def Leppard tee shirt who pulled in the big grouper that Roger hung because Roger was almost pulled overboard. Then the first mate brought some filets packed in ice to Roger's motel door because Roger was ill with sunburn and still seasick.

Roger had been paying money all day for everything and so when he went to bed, ill, he inserted a quarter for the Magic Fingers.

Something went wrong.

The bed tossed around worse than the boat in four feet of waves.

There was vomit all over the room and when Roger woke up, hearing the knock on the door, he opened the ice chest and looked at the big grouper filets and before he could do anything about it, he threw up on the fish, too, reeling blindly and full of bile back to the bed, which was still on, bucking. His wife was still asleep—but when she heard the new retching sounds from Roger, him trying to lie down, she thought something amorous was up and would have gone for him except for the filthy smell he had.

She crawled away.

Mrs. Reba Laird was a fine woman from Georgia, with her body in trim. She had looked up the origin of the Laird name. In Scots, it means landholder. She knew there was an aristocratic past to her husband, for she herself had found out that her side of the family were thieves and murderers brought over by Ogle-thorpe to populate and suffer from the jungles of Georgia. She thought Roger was a wonderful lover when he wasn't fishing.

Roger eschewed freshwater fishing in Louisiana, where the Lairds lived now, except for the giant cat-fish in a river near the Texas border. He got a stout pole, a big hook, and let it down weighted with ocean lead and a large wounded shad. He had read all the fishing tips in *Field & Stream* and he knew those giants were down there because there were other men fishing right where he was with stiff rods and wounded live shad.

The man to Roger's right hooked into one and it

was a tussle, tangling all the lines out—so Roger felt the mother down there, all right.

When they got the fish out, by running a jeep in and hooking the line to the bumper, it was the weight of ninety pounds.

The jeep backed over Roger's brand-new fishing rod and snapped it into two pieces and ground his fishing reel into the deep muck. Roger saw the fish and watched them wrench it up, hanging from the back bar of the jeep. He was amazed and excited—but the fish was not his. Still, he photographed it with his Polaroid. But when Roger added up the day, it had cost him close to three hundred dollars for a Polaroid picture.

The thing about it was that Roger was not dumb. He was handsome, slender, gray at the temples, with his forehair receding to reveal an intelligent cranium, nicely shaped like that of a tanned, professional fisherman.

Roger watched the Southern teevee shows about fishing—Bill Dance, others—and he had read the old Jason Lucas books, wherein Lucas claims he can catch fish under any conditions, even chopping holes in the ice in Wisconsin at a chill degree of minus fifty and taking his limit in walleye and muskie. Also, Roger had read Izaak Walton, but he had no use for England and all that olden shit.

It was a big saltwater one he wanted, around the Gulf of Mexico where he lived. On the flats near Isamodorado, Roger had hung a big bonefish. However, he was alone and it dragged the skiff into some branches where there were several heavy cottonmouth moccasins.

He reached for the pistol in his kit. One of the snakes, with its mouth open, had fallen in the boat. Roger shot the stern floor out of the boat. As the boat sank, all his expensive gear in it, Roger Laird kept going down, reloading, firing at the trees, and when he went underwater he thought he saw the big bonefish under the water, which was later, as he recalled, a Florida gar. He could see underwater and could hold his breath underwater and was, withal, in good shape. But the .25 automatic shot underwater rather startled the ears, and the bullet went out in slow motion like a lead pellet thrown left-handed by a sissy. So Roger waded out of the water, still firing a few rounds to keep Nature away from him. Then got his wind back and dove in to recover his radio.

The Coast Guard came and got him.

Roger's father, Bill Laird, was a tender traveler of eighty years in his new Olds 98. Old Mr. Laird found remarkable animals all over the land. Behind a service station in Bastrop, Louisiana, he saw a dog playing with a robin. The two of them were friends, canine and bird. They had been friends a long time. Grievously, one day the dog became too rough and killed the bird. The men at the service station were sort of in mourning. They stared at the nacreous eyes of the bird on the counter. The dog was under the counter, looking up sorrowfully at the corpse.

Nothing of this should have occurred.

Roger thought of his father, who had always loved animal life and was quite a scholar on the habits of anything on land that roved on four legs.

Well, where was Roger now?

Roger was at Mexico Beach, thirty miles south of

Panama City. He was out of money and had brought only a Zebco 33 with a stiff fiberglass rod. He had no money for bait, and he was just helping pay some of the groceries for George and Anna Lois and their son and stepdaughter, who had a baby. The house was old and wooden, with a screen porch running around two sides; a splendid beach house owned by Slade West, a veteran of Normandy, who had once kept a pet lion there. The lion started chasing cars when the Florida boom hit, and he had to give it to a zoo.

At the moment, Roger was alone in the house. He was looking out over the ocean at some crows. The crows hung around, although it was not their place. They fetched and quacked in the air and were rolled by sea breezes off the mark.

Somebody's dog from down the way came in and rolled privately in the sea oats. What a lark, all to himself, he was having! Feet in the air and twisting his back in the sand and the roots! But the heavy dangerous trucks going by were just feet from the dog. The dog was playing it very close.

Yesterday, Roger had caught a crab on his line that reminded him of himself. The crab was ageing well and, dumb as hell, was holding on till the very, very last, where Roger might drag him in out of the water if he wanted him. The crab was in the surf, clamped on the shrimp and hook, trying to prove something. While the crab was looking at Roger and deciding on the moment, the dog dashed into the water and tore the crab to pieces with its jaws.

Roger had never seen anything like this. Not only was Roger stunned, he had now caught a dog! So he ran down the beach lickety-split with a loose line—so the hook wouldn't hurt the dog's lips. Roger offered abject apologies, pulling the last ten from his wallet to pay the vet bill.

Next door to the house where Roger was staying was an ugly little brick house fenced in as if somebody would want to take something from it. The owner and occupant was a Mr. Mintner, possibly a vampire. Roger had never seen Mr. Mintner come out into the sun and all the plant signs around the house were dead and dry. Parked outside was a Harley Davidson golf cart, and at 11 p.m. three nights ago Roger had seen Mr. Mintner crank up the golf cart and come back from the Minute Market with several bloody-looking steaks and beef bouillon cubes and some radishes. Roger saw all this in the dim outside light of Mr. Mintner's. He saw Mr. Mintner in a black golf outfit and black boots, and his arms were pale almost to luminescence. There was a story that his heart had been broken by a woman years ago and that he had never recovered.

Roger had a fascinated aversion to this Mintner and believed that he should be hauled away and made to eat with accountants.

Roger, with no financial resources at the time, cleaned up the house and read some of the *National Geographic*s and *Discover* magazines around the place. He had brought along his fisherman's log, in which there was not one entry, only some notes on the last pages where it said NOTES.

He looked out at the green softly rolling ocean again. There were a lot of things out there in "the big pond," as McClane's *New Standard Fishing Encyclopedia* called the Gulf. There were things like marlin and sailfish and cobia/ling and bluefish. As for the little ocean catfish, Roger had caught his weight twenty times over of them.

They were trash and insignificant.

Today George and his son Steve were out casting in the surf and catching some small whiting. Roger waded into the water, feeling the warm wash over his sneakers, and then stood straddle legged, arms behind his back, rather like a taller Napoléon surveying an opposing infantry horde from an unexpected country of idiots.

Two-thirds of the world was water, wasn't it?

There were king mackerel out there, too, and big snapper. But Roger had no funds to hire a boat, and all his wonderful gear was back in Louisiana in his garage, every line coiled perfectly, every hook on every lure honed to surgical sharpness, every reel oiled and soundless. As for what Roger had here at Mexico Beach, it was the cheap Zebco with a light-medium–weight rod, the whole thing coming out of a plastic package from T G & Y at a price of twenty-four dollars—such a rig as you would buy a nephew on his eleventh birthday.

Roger's friend George Epworth was having a good time with his son Steve. They were up to their hips in water, casting away with shrimp on the hook. They caught a ground mullet, which Roger inspected. This kind of mullet is not the leaping vegetarian that is caught with a net only. Roger looked on with pursed lips. Then there were some croakers, who gave them a little tussle. It was fine kid sport, with the surf break-ing right around the armpits of the fellows. Steve's wife, Becky, had made a tent over their baby, and

Anna Lois, newly a grandmother, was watching the baby and reading from one of Slade West's encyclopedias of sea life. George was a biochemist back at Millsaps College in Jackson. Anna Lois worked for the state crime lab, and their ocean time was precious. They liked *everything* out here and knew a good bit about sea chemistry. Roger envied them somewhat. But he had only a fever for the big one, the one to write home about, the one to stuff, varnish, and mount, whereas none of these fish were approaching a pound, though they were beautiful.

Roger was wondering what in the deuce was so *wrong* with him and his luck now.

Not just the fish.

Not just the fact that his Reba had gone a bit nuts when menopause came on her.

Not just the fact that she bought a new dress *every* day, and from high-priced boutiques, and that she stayed in the bathroom for an hour, making up—but that she emerged in earrings and hose and high heels only to sit on the couch and stare at the wall across from her. Not at a mirror, not at a picture, not at the television, not smoking anymore, not drinking, not reading—which she had loved—just sitting there with a little grieving smile on her face. She wasn't grouchy. She just sat, staring with the startling big gray eyes that had charmed Roger to raving for her back in college days. They'd just had their twenty-fifth anniversary, Roger and Reba.

Further, his luck with money recently. Why, he'd had near a hundred-fifty thousand in the bank, and they were thinking about living on interest for the first time ever when *bang*, the offshore-drilling speculation in which they had the stock exploded and the money was gone.

It made Roger so tired he had not the energy to track down the reasons.

As for Nature, Roger was tiring, too. He had a weary alliance with Nature—the roses, the wisteria, and the cardinals and the orioles and the raccoons round the deck on the rear of his dutch-roofed little castle. But he was not charmed much now when he went out there and looked.

Were his senses shutting down? He who had never had to use even reading glasses and about whom everyone said he looked a decade younger than he was? At least?

Roger Laird was about to turn and go back to his room, shut the curtains, write in his fishing log *something* that might give him an idea as to what was wrong with him, when something happened out beyond the breakers.

He saw it roll, and he saw a fin of some kind stand up.

Then it rolled again!

A rising shower of small fish leapt up and the gulls hurried over, seconded by the crows, quacking but not knowing how to work the sea as the gulls did.

The big fin came up again!

Roger's eyes narrowed and the point of his vision met on the swirl of water as if on the wrong end of a pair of Zeisses. Given the swirl, the fish was seven to nine feet long at the smallest.

Roger looked slyly around to see if any of his friends, the Epworths, had noticed it. But they were otherwise occupied and had not.

Roger looked again, bending as if to find a nice conch shell like a lady tourist, and the thing rolled again!

The birds were snapping the moiling little minnows, the crows missing and having to move out heavy on the flap because of their sogged feathers.

Then there was no activity.

Roger walked back with the Epworths, helping to carry the bucket of fish they intended to roast over charcoal for lunch. The baby was put to bed. Steve and his wife lay on the divan watching the soap opera "General Hospital." The local weather and fishing report came on. The man with big spectacles said the weather was fine but the fishing was no good, apologizing to the world for the ocean this week.

After they had eaten the smoked fish and salad and the oysters Rockefeller, everybody was sleepy except Roger—who pretended sleepiness and went to his room. It was a half hour he waited there, studying the Zebco outfit in the corner. Then you could hear nothing in the house, and he, despite himself, began making phony snoring noises.

Barefooted, he scooted to the kitchen and found the plastic bowl of bait shrimp. He eased the door to, not even the sound of a vacuum sucking on rubber. Then he put on his sneakers and, holding the Zebco unit, he slipped out into the driveway.

Roger was about halfway down the drive, aiming straight for the sea, when a loud voice from the little ugly red brick house horrified him.

"*You!*"

It was Mr. Mintner, shouting from his window.

The pale man was holding the windowsill, speaking with his nose practically against the screen.

"Getting any?" shouted Mintner.

There was a horrifying derisive laugh, like rolling tin, and then the window came down with a smash, Mintner receding into the dark of the room. It was two in the afternoon and the house was totally unlit.

Roger was not certain that there had been a man at all. Perhaps it was just a voice giving body to something waxen and then vanishing.

He had never been a coward. But he was unsettled when he reached the sea. He had some trouble tying on the hook. It was not even a sea hook. It was a thin golden bass hook that came with the Zebco kit. He put the bell weight on and looked out, yearning at the blue-gray hole where the creature had shown.

There was not a bird in sight. There was no whirl and leaping of minnows. The water was as dead as a pond some bovine might be drinking from.

Roger stayed near the water—waiting, getting ready.

Then he cast—a nice long cast—easy with this much lead on the line, and the rig plumped down within a square yard of where he'd seen the fish.

He tightened the line and waited.

There was a tug but small and he knew it was a crab. He jerked the line back, cursing, and reeled in. The shrimp was gone. He looked in the plastic bowl and got the biggest shrimp there, peeled it, and ran it onto the hook, so that his bait looked like a succulent question mark almost to the geometry.

This time he threw long but badly, way over to one side.

It didn't matter.

He knew it didn't matter. He was just hoping that that crab-eating dog wouldn't show up, and he hadn't even tightened his line when it hit.

It was big and it was on.

He could not budge it, and he knew he'd snap the line if he tried.

He forgot how the drag worked. He forgot everything. Everything went into a hot rapid glared picture, and he was yanked into the sea, past his knees, up to his waist, then floundering, swimming, struggling up.

Then he began running knee-deep and following the fish.

Jesus—oh, thank you, please, please, yes—holy Christ, it was coming toward him now! He reeled in rapidly. He had gone yards and yards down the beach.

It came on in. He could pull it in. It was coming. It was bending the rod double. But it was coming. He had it. Just not be dumb and lose it.

It surfaced. A sand shark. About four feet long and fifteen pounds. But Roger had never seen anything so lovely and satisfying. He grabbed the line and hauled it toward him, and there it was, white bellied and gray topped, and now he had it on the sand and it was *his*, looking like a smiling tender rocket from the deep, a fish so young, so handsome, so perfect for its business, and so unlucky.

By this time a crowd had gathered, and Roger was on his knees in the sand, sweating profusely and with his chest full of such good air it was like a gas of silver in him.

The crowd began saying things.

"I'll kill him with this flounder gig! Everybody stand back!" said one of the young men.

"Ooo! Ugg!" said a young somebody else.

George Epworth was on the beach by then.

"That was something. I watched you through the binoculars. That was something." George Epworth knelt and watched the shark heaving away.

"Would you unhook him for me?" Roger Laird asked.

George Epworth reached down, cut the line, and pulled the hook out backward through the shank, leaving only a tiny hole.

A man who had been cutting up drift logs for a fire said, "I'll do the honors. They're good to eat, you know."

The man was raising his axe and waiting for Roger to move away.

"Not mine, you don't!" Roger screamed, and then he picked up the shark by the tail and threw it way out in the water. It turned over on its back and washed in as if dying for a few minutes, whereupon it flipped over and eased into the deep green.

When Roger Laird got back to Louisiana, he did not know what kind of story to tell. He only knew that his lungs were full of the exquisite silvery gas.

Reba Laird became better. They were bankrupt, had to sell the little castle with the dutch roof. She couldn't buy any more dresses or jewelry. But she smiled at Roger Laird. No more staring at the wall.

He sold all his fishing gear at a terrible loss, and they moved to Dallas, address unknown.

Then Roger Laird made an old-fashioned two-by-four pair of stilts eight feet high. It made him stand about twelve feet in the air. He would mount the stilts and walk into the big lake around which the rich people lived. The sailing boats would come around near him, big opulent three-riggers sleeping two families belowdecks, and Roger Laird would yell:

"Fuck you! Fuck you!"

Idaho

These guys are, some of them, descendants of runaway Confederate troops from Arkansas and Texas. They didn't want any more of the war and rode, rode, straggled, gasped, into the Northwest Territory. Their tired horses and frightened families rested under the big sky, under the big mountains.

But I had a job in Montana at the college in Missoula. On this campus you will see the impressive bronze emblem of the college, a statue of a grizzly bear in motion. It is a shame that while I was in Montana I never saw a live grizzly in person. But I saw people.

The people, even in the English department, were friendly and capacious. University of Montana was the place to be. You saw the usual drudges working with computers against Shakespeare, but there were joys in looking in faces that would look right back at you. I found the students refreshingly adventurous and pretty. Shall I say they lacked the smugness?

I lived across from the post office on Patee Street.

The number in Patee Street was the number of my old address in Alabama, and Patty was the name of my second and last wife. She was the one I loved to absolute despair.

Just curious, it was, all this. No magic, please, no preforeordestination.

The magic comes from the surrounding softly rolling brown smooth hills around Missoula. You wake every day held in the palm of the valley between those hills.

Pretty soon I had a girl named Anne—Italian from New York. She chattered like a toy with all its Italo-American past on tape. She was inquisitive and exhilarated about everything, especially about Montana, about just the name for starters, and she was sweet and full of presents and bountiful of breast, with a slightly witchlike nose saved by the deep brown eyes of a six-year-old.

I began drinking and playing pool and winning some money—and my life was bursting with a heroic certainty. I danced, as I do not when sober, and I was fond of my friends and of my new dog, Jill. Because I had been lonely for a while in my little apartment, really ghastly lonely—missing my kids and the South and my girl, Teresa—I bought Jill from Petland for thirty dollars, which is what I did even though there were no dogs allowed at my place.

When it began snowing, I'd walk Jill around the block to Butterfly Herb's, where I calmly drank coffee and pretended I was not hung over, trembling and buying every vitamin and herb in the store. I knew I was going to keep this one going. I was going to stay with white russians and keep this one going, going into the snow, ice, and mud—the very color of my drink.

Sometimes I was sober and borrowed a graduate student's BMW bike and Anne and I would ride over on toward Idaho, past Fort Fizzle, where the U.S. Cavalry was made a fool of by Chief Joseph of the Nez Percé, who simply walked his tribe around the fort and ignored it. We rode out of Lolo and across the pass. The road rose and the temp dropped. I was taking the old BMW motorcycle along—1960 model —and trying to be the hero in my leather jacket. But it got cold and I couldn't stand it and I stopped at a country-log kind of store, where the folks were friendly but mainly warm. Lodge pine, I guess they called it; my hands still clutched to the handlebars and I walked through the store casually getting nearer the heater. When I was warmer, I bought an Idaho patch for my jacket and have ever since lied about seeing Idaho.

Hence we descended back to Missoula, descending back to the spreading paper mill city of Missoula, over the bridge of the river and to my place with its flat blue rugs, looking right out on the post office, the Federal Building, and the IRS and the enlistment and all that. As I write now, I still owe the IRS, and they've levied my salary and my writing money and they get all the money I get from this. And I am writing because I don't owe anything except writing.

But here is the real story, and the story is about my friendship with Richard Hugo, the poet. For, after all, I had gone out to Montana mainly to meet Richard Hugo, and to pal around with my buddies Tom and

Laurie McGuane over in the Paradise Valley near Livingston.

The McGuanes, I'd met them when Tom called from the Ramada Inn when I was at my hometown of Clinton, Mississippi. He and Laurie were riding in a cutting-horse competition in Jackson. Tom called to say he liked my writing and wanted me to know it. They were eight miles away, and I got in my mother's Cadillac and proceeded over to the Ramada, where eventually I saw the radiant black-haired Laurie mount her steed, one of these cutting horses that are quarter horses trained to pick out a diseased or significant stray cow from the herd. One of them, Tom told me, was worth five million dollars. I was awed, especially since I was broke and with no prospects. But even more awed was I by Laurie, riding the horse on the sawdust, in her high boots and her smart hat.

The contest was quiet—really very quiet, for so many animals around—and I hadn't quite got the hang of it. Eventually I brought my kids over and we sat on the bleachers with hot dogs and popcorn and Cokes. I was looking on as innocent as you can look. Later, my nephew Taylor and I ate at the George Street Grocery with the McGuanes, who had their new baby Annie with them. Oh, it was wonderful. McGuane is a giant in heart and body, and where are you giants anymore?

But to get back to Richard Hugo, he was dying when I met him in his office. I did not know it. He looked a bit hung over, I thought. A little pressed for time. Not only did I think his poetry was straight, clear, and full, I knew that he had helped me get the job in Montana by dispelling the talk that I had pulled a gun on a class of writing students in Alabama. Responsible for this rumor are enemies that I will see to in the future. Anyway, Hugo had told them I had fired a pistol through the floorboards of my car to let some rainwater out, which was true.

Then I read his "Letter" poems and saw what could be done with honest sentiment. I saw him only two whole times. The last time he was huffing and puffing toward the down stairway and in a hurry. I knew he'd had one lung removed, and with his weight, I didn't think his breathing was past normal. He said he was on his way to the doctor. The next thing he was dead of cancer in a hospital.

There was the ceremony, at which his favorite tunes were played and his old friends—barkeeps and a dockworker and a freshly sober writer or two, plus his stepson, gave short testimony to his life. Hugo was a fisher for trout, with worms from a lawn-chair. He would fish in the rain, and he would fish from his Buick convertible.

The best speaker, I thought, was an old Seattle friend of his named Johnny, who appeared in a suit and tie. He was stumpy, red faced and had white cropped hair. He told a story about a man faced with the possibility of moving a 125,000-ton boat out of a dock—single-handedly, manually, no motor. It could not be done, of course. The man stared at the project and stared. Before the day was over, he pushed the barge out into the harbor with his back and legs alone.

Then this Johnny broke down into some manly weeping.

"And that's what Dick did with his education and his poetry," said Johnny.

I began tearing up, and though I never knew Dick Hugo, really, never heard him read his poems, and though I had no claim to being a buddy of his, I knew an immense something, like that barge in Johnny's speech, had moved away from me and was hugely and cumbersomely cutting the water now, having been pushed out by hand.

Then I got myself back in my room and began sorting my tapes, and there was all of Jimi Hendrix. I mean all. I wear a Hendrix patch on my right sleeve on my leathers. I don't think Dick Hugo would have liked Jimi's music, though they are from the same town. I was wild in my sorrow and my separation from my children. I was stepping away from that slobbering thug, self-pity. I thought I would try to. Truth is, the drunk has all the feeling for the miracle and not quite the substance of it. He is apt for the miracle. What you like about the one nice snap in the blood is the hope for the big thing. And then you are greedy for the miracle. It is too good, this closeness, and you want to go on over, across the river and into the trees with Stonewall Jackson, who refused liquor because he liked it too much. At the big battle, he sucked a lemon all day—suck, suck—while his foot cavalry hit and hit again.

When I got back here to Mississippi, I got out my old collection of family guns and those I'd acquired. I oiled them. I used the Genuine Old English cherry-smelling furniture polish on the stocks.

My kids were around me, and I was sober and happy. I displayed the guns proudly. I had their butts resting on a camel saddle I'd got in one of the Missoula pawnshops. So they were all oiled and imposing. And then they were fairly promptly stolen by some black guys working for me.

I was angry and started using the word *nigger* a great deal, this time meaning it with real nastiness in my heart. But it's all right now. I shoot Coke cans with a pistol I still got out in the country. I listen to the birds in the early morning, no other sound in the house.

My woman Margaret's here. She plays the flute so sweetly and lushly. She's just about to join the birds of nature.

I look down at my hand. It's not a gun. It's only a pencil. I am not going anywhere.

I Am Shaking to Death

We went over there, Nag and I, because of nothing else to do over here, and there were things going on, all right. A man had a fat farm south of town way out in the sticks, near Yocona or something like that. It was not spoken of too generally. What a wretched, hot buggy piece of the South it was down there, the remnants of horse country, they said. There never was any good farming there. Man had a fat farm that was somewhat illegal.

The fat women were tied to a rope behind a jeep, naked, and he would, or somebody would, drive them slow down through a long pasture and into a swamp like so much, what can I say, head of pork, except they agreed to it, the women I mean, from the North, the far North, the East, not just the South. They agreed that they were ugly enough for things to happen to them and they would not be released until they were thin and better. And when they were thin, their attitudes had improved and they could leave or not, but you bet they were changed. So we would wait out there watching them and slowly fall in love with one or two.

In the heat and the bugs, they clambered along mud-spattered behind the jeep, none of them looking like a panty ad, not yet, sliding through gook and briars. We thought—at least I did—about women and their burdens, these burdens of fat they had brought on themselves. And it was quite a joy to watch them struggle for relief.

It became August, and I saw on the steps of the Episcopal Church her, the one I'd had my eye on.

I went up to introduce myself.

She was in a black silk dress with black shoes and slim calves. I guess we fell in love with each other.

For after church, on Sunday afternoons, she would come by my place and I would press her and press her. She would undress, and I would press her and press her.

How can I forget the joy that a lean woman offers you, her brown legs raised for your giant urgency, her one stocking still on one leg, she wants you so much. And she tells you do it, do it, and then yes, more.

Some women you don't like after you've exhausted yourself in her, like you're both out on the meat rack at the Jitney Jungle—it's already dead and the less said the better.

But this woman was not some women.

She said nothing. She just smiled and was quiet; I admired the way she was graceful putting back on her hose and shoes and stepped back in her dress. She left off the brassiere because she saw me looking at her breasts again, and they were miraculous.

This woman I had watched lean down from something near porcine, a nameless drudge in a group of them, to something you just had to see—oh, my.

She addressed her hair in the bathroom. I've got a nice place with all sorts of mirrors. Mainly to remind me of who I am.

I am trying to get better looking and wiser as I age, just like everybody my age I know. Even trying to quit the cigarettes and the beer.

There is a guy in town, black. I lent him my car and he stole it. He professed to me that he was my friend, a brother, and then he stole my Cutlass. I'll never get over how slim, soft-spoken, and well-dressed he was.

He was missing his upper teeth.

I thought I could trust a guy with his upper teeth already gone.

They found him over in the Senatobia Jail. I myself was once locked in there one night for DWI. It's a horrible place. The jailors watch teevee and forget you ever occurred. Then they all get together and lie when you try to get some justice.

So that's what she and I began talking about, she with a strawberry cotton dress on this time. She said almost nothing, her eyes just glittering blue and her white nice teeth and the pink full lips.

"I guess you've got it made," she said at last, looking around at my place, all my art on the walls and my Scandinavian furniture.

"In the shade," I said.

The air-conditioner was pumping and that was all we could hear for about five minutes.

"Well," she said, "I don't, I don't at all. I spent just about my last dime getting this way. I don't have even the fare back to Minneapolis."

I took us in the Jaguar up to Minneapolis. We tried to stay along the river because the water always gives me peace. I like to get my Jag dirty-looking at the river and hear on my tape deck some old Sam and Dave songs. The Jag is an orchestra inside.

We got out and danced on the levee, shoes muddy, tires muddy.

Then I pressed her in the snow and she pressed me back. Then we went back into the motel in lower Minnesota and it was cold. I was shivering so much we almost had to call somebody. She couldn't get all the quilts on me fast enough, and I stood up, six-feet-four, skinny legs, long hair frozen and clacking around my eyes blind with cold, and I was shaking and shaking. Out the window the moon sat down in front of my eyes and looked at me with all its scars on it—no clouds, nothing, a white horror without a face. I mean, no features except that acne it has.

When I finally got warmer, I still had nothing to say. She ordered some soup, and my teeth and throat shot it all over her.

Her. The one I loved.

Anything. Help. I am shaking to death.

Her home was even farther north!

We went into Minneapolis, the city. But I forgot.

When people say they live in a city up North, you still have miles to travel—and then, and then. Even the Jag was complaining about the cold and the distance and then there was still more of it ahead.

I don't remember her house. Like me, she owned too much.

I really wish she'd read this and write me a letter.

Even Greenland

I was sitting radar. Actually doing nothing.

We had been up to seventy-five thousand to give the afternoon some jazz. I guess we were still in Mexico, coming into Miramar eventually in the F-14. It doesn't much matter after you've seen the curvature of the earth. For a while, nothing much matters at all. We'd had three sunsets already. I guess it's what you'd call really living the day.

But then,

"John," said I, "this plane's on fire."

"I know it," he said.

John was sort of short and angry about it.

"You thought of last-minute things any?" said I.

"Yeah. I ran out of a couple of things already. But they were cold, like. They didn't catch the moment. Bad writing," said John.

"You had the advantage. You've been knowing," said I.

"Yeah. I was going to get a leap on you. I was going to smoke you. Everything you said, it wasn't

31

going to be good enough. I was going to have a great one, and everything you said, it wasn't going to be good enough," said he.

"But it's not like that," said I. "Is it?"

He said, "Nah. I got nothing, really."

The wings were turning red. I guess you'd call it red. It was a shade against dark blue that was mystical flamingo, very spaceylike, like living blood. Was the plane bleeding?

"You have a good time in Peru?" said I.

"Not really," said John. "I got something to tell you. I haven't had a 'good time' in a long time. There's something between me and a good time since, I don't know, since I was twenty-eight or like that. I've seen a lot, but you know I haven't quite *seen* it. Like somebody's seen it already. It wasn't fresh. There were eyes that had used it up some."

"Even high in Mérida?" said I.

"Even," said John.

"Even Tibet, where you met your wife. By accident a beautiful American girl way up there?" said I.

"Even," said John.

"Even Greenland?" said I.

John said, "Yes. Even Greenland. It's fresh, but it's not fresh. There are footsteps in the snow."

"Maybe," said I, "you think about in Mississippi when it snows, when you're a kid. And you're the first up and there's been nobody in the snow, no footsteps."

"Shut up," said John.

"Look, are we getting into a fight here at the moment of death? We going to mix it up with the plane's on fire?"

"Shut up! Shut up!" said John. Yelled John.

"What's wrong?" said I.

He wouldn't say anything. He wouldn't budge at the controls. We might burn but we were going to hold level. We weren't seeking the earth at all.

"What is it, John?" said I.

John said, "You son of a bitch, that was *mine*— that snow in Mississippi. Now it's all shot to shit."

The paper from his kneepad was flying all over the cockpit, and I could see his hand flapping up and down with the pencil in it, angry.

"It was mine, *mine*, you rotten cocksucker! You see what I mean?"

The little pages hung up on the top, and you could see the big moon just past them.

"Eject! Save your ass!" said John.

But I said, "What about you, John?"

John said, "I'm staying. Just let me have *that* one, will you?"

"But you can't," said I.

But he did.

Celeste and I visit the burn on the blond sand under one of those black romantic worthless mountains five miles or so out from Miramar base.

I am a lieutenant commander in the reserve now. But to be frank, it shakes me a bit even to run a Skyhawk up to Malibu and back.

Celeste and I squat in the sand and say nothing as we look at the burn. They got all the metal away.

I don't know what Celeste is saying or thinking, I am so absorbed myself and paralyzed.

I know I am looking at John's damned triumph.

Ride, Fly, Penetrate, Loiter

My name is Ned Maximus, but they call me Maximum Ned.

Three years ago, when I was a drunk, a hitch-hiker stabbed me in the eye with my own filet knife. I wear a patch on the right one now. It was a fake Indian named Billy Seven Fingers. He was having the shakes, and I was trying to get him to the bootleggers off the reservation in Neshoba County, Mississippi. He was white as me—whiter, really, because I have some Spanish.

He asked me for another cigarette, and I said no, that's too many, and besides you're a fake—you might be gouging the Feds with thirty-second-part maximum Indian blood, but you don't fool me.

I had only got to the *maximum* part when he was on my face with the fish knife out of the pocket of the MG Midget.

There were three of us. Billy Seven Fingers was sitting on the lap of his enormous sick real Indian friend. They had been drinking Dr. Tichenors antiseptic in Philadelphia, and I picked them up sick at five in the morning, working on my Johnnie Walker Black.

The big Indian made the car seem like a toy. Then we got out in the pines, and the last thing of any note I saw with my right eye was a Dalmatian dog run out near the road, and this was wonderful in rural Mississippi—practically a miracle—it was truth and beauty like John Keats has in that poem. And I wanted a dog to redeem my life as drunks and terrible women do.

But they wouldn't help me chase it. They were too sick.

So I went on, pretty dreadfully let down. It was the best thing offering lately.

I was among dwarves over in Alabama at the school, where almost everybody dies early. There is a poison in Tuscaloosa that draws souls toward the low middle. Hardly anybody has honest work. Queers full of backbiting and rumors set the tone. Nobody has ever missed a meal. Everybody has about exactly enough courage to jaywalk or cheat a wife or a friend with a quote from Nietzsche on his lips.

Thus it seemed when I was a drunk, raving with bad attitudes. I drank and smiled and tried to love, wanting some hero for a buddy: somebody who would attack the heart of the night with me. I had worn out all the parlor charity of my wife. She was doing the standard frigid lockout at home, enjoying my trouble and her cold rectitude. The drunkard lifts sobriety into a great public virtue in the smug and snakelike heart. It may be his major service. Thus it seemed when I was a drunk, raving with bad attitudes.

So there I was, on my knees in the pebble dust on the shoulder of the road, trying to get the pistol out of the trunk of my car.

An eye is a beautiful thing! I shouted.

An eye is a beautiful thing!

I was howling and stumbling.

You frauding ugly shit! I howled.

But they were out of the convertible and away. My fingers were full of blood, but it didn't hurt that much. When I finally found the gun, I fired it everywhere and went out with a white heat of loud horror.

I remember wanting a drink terribly in the emergency room. I had the shakes. And then I was in another room and didn't. My veins were warm with dope, the bandage on. But another thing—there was my own personal natural dope running in me. My head was very high and warm. I was exhilarated, in fact. I saw with penetrating clarity with my lone left eye.

It has been so ever since. Except the dead one has come alive and I can see the heart of the night with it. It throws a grim net sometimes, but I am lifted up.

Nowadays this is how it goes with me: ride, fly, penetrate, loiter.

I left Tuscaloosa—the hell with Tuscaloosa—on a Triumph motorcycle black and chrome. My hair was long, leather on my loins, bandana of the forehead in place, standard dope-drifter gear, except for the bow and arrows strapped on the sissy bar.

No guns.

Guns are for cowards.

But the man who comes near my good eye will walk away a spewing porcupine.

The women of this town could beg and beg, but I would never make whoopee with any of them again.

Thus it seemed when I was a drunk.

I was thirty-eight and somewhat Spanish. I could make a stand in this chicken house no longer.

Now I talk white, Negro, some Elizabethan, some Apache. My dark eye pierces and writhes and brings up odd talk in me sometimes. Under the patch, it burns deep for language. I will write sometimes and my bones hurt. I believe heavily in destiny at such moments.

I went in a bar in Dallas before the great ride over the desert that I intended. I had not drunk for a week. I took some water and collected the past. I thought of my books, my children, and the fact that almost everybody sells used cars or dies early. I used to get so angry about this issue that I would drag policemen out of their cars. I fired an arrow through the window of my last wife's, hurting nothing but the cozy locked glass and disturbing the sleep of grown children.

It was then I took the leap into the wasteland, happy as Brer Rabbit in the briars. That long long, bloated epicene tract "The Waste Land" by Eliot—

the slide show of some snug librarian on the rag—was nothing, unworthy, in the notes that every sissy throws away. I would not talk to students about it. You throw it down like a pickled egg with nine Buds and move on to giving it to the preacher's wife on a hill while she spits on a photograph of her husband.

I began on the Buds, but I thought I was doing better. The standard shrill hag at the end of the bar had asked me why I did not have a ring in my ear, and I said nothing at all. Hey, pirate! she was shrieking when I left, ready to fire out of Dallas. But I went back toward Louisiana, my home state, Dallas had sickened me so much.

Dallas, city of the fur helicopters. Dallas—computers, plastics, urban cowboys with schemes and wolf shooting in their hearts. The standard artist for Dallas should be Mickey Gilley, a studied fraud who might well be singing deeply about ripped fiberglass. His cousin is Jerry Lee Lewis, still very much from Louisiana. The Deep South might be wretched, but it can howl.

I went back to the little town in the pines near Alexandria where I grew up. I didn't even visit my father, just sat on my motorcycle and stared at the little yellow store. At that time I had still not forgiven him for converting to Baptist after Mother's death.

I had no real home at all then, and I looked in the dust at my boots, and I considered the beauty of my black and chrome Triumph 650 Twin, 73 model, straight pipes to horrify old hearts, electricity by

Lucas. I stepped over to the porch, unsteady, to get more beer, and there she was with her white luggage, Celeste, the one who would be a movie star, a staggering screen vision that every sighted male who saw the cinema would wet the sheets for.

I walked by her, and she looked away, because I guess I looked pretty rough. I went on in the store—and now I can tell you, this is what I saw when my dead eye went wild. I have never been the same since.

The day is so still, it is almost an object. The rain will not come. The clouds are white, burned high away.

On the porch of the yellow store, in her fresh stockings despite the heat, her toes eloquent in the white straps of her shoes, the elegant young lady waits. The men, two of them, look out to her occasionally. In the store, near a large reservoir, hang hooks, line, Cheetos, prophylactics, cream nougats. The roof of the store is tin. Around the woman the men, three decades older, see hot love and believe they can hear it speak from her ankles.

They cannot talk. Their tongues are thick. Flies mount their shoulders and cheeks, but they don't go near her, her bare shoulders wonderful above her sundress. She wears earrings, ivory dangles, and when she moves, looking up the road, they swing and kiss her shoulders almost, and the heat ripples about but it does not seem to touch her, and she is not of this place, and there is no earthly reason.

The men in the store are stunned. They have forgotten how to move, what to say. Her beauty. The two white leather suitcases on either side of her.

"My wife is a withered rag," one man suddenly blurts to the other.

"Life here is a belligerent sow, not a prayer," responds the other.

The woman has not heard all they say to each other. But she's heard enough. She knows a high point is near, a declaration.

"This store fills me with dread. I have bleeding needs," says the owner.

"I suck a dry dug daily," says the other. "There's grease from nothing, just torpor, in my fingernails."

"My God, for relief from this old charade, my mercantilia!"

"There is a bad God," groans the other, pounding a rail. "The story is riddled with holes."

The woman hears a clatter around the counter. One of the men, the owner, is moving. He reaches for a can of snuff. The other casts himself against a bare spar in the wall. The owner is weeping outright.

He spits into the snuff in his hands. He thrusts his hands into his trousers, plunging his palms to his groin. The other man has found a length of leather and thrashes the wall, raking his free hand over a steel brush. He snaps the brush to his forehead. He spouts choked groans, gasping sorrows. The two of them upset goods, shatter the peace of the aisles. The man with the leather removes his shoes. He removes a shovel from its holder, punches it at his feet, howls and reattacks his feet angrily, crying for his mute heels.

"My children are low-hearted fascists! Their eye-brows meet! The oldest boy's in San Diego, but he's a pig! We're naught but dying animals. Eve and then Jesus and us, clerks!"

The owner jams his teeth together, and they crack. He pushes his tongue out, evicting a rude air sound. The other knocks over a barrel of staves.

"Lost! Oh, lost!" the owner spouts. "The redundant dusty clock of my tenure here!"

"Ah, heart pie!" moans the other.

The woman casts a glance back.

A dog has been aroused and creeps out from its bin below the counter. The owner slays the dog with repeated blows of the shovel, lifting fur into the air in great gouts.

She, Celeste, looks cautiously ahead. The road is still empty.

The owner has found some steep plastic sandals and is wearing them—jerking, breaking wind, and opening old sores. He stomps at imagined miniature men on the floor. The sound—the snorts, cries, rebuffs, indignant grunts—is unsettling.

The woman has a quality about her. That and the heat.

I have been sober ever since.

I have just told a lie.

At forty, I am at a certain peace. I have plenty of money and the love of a beautiful red-haired girl from Colorado. What's more, the closeness with my children has come back to a heavenly beauty, each child a hero better than yours.

You may see me with the eye-patch, though, in almost any city of the South, the Far West, or the Northwest. I am on the black and chrome Triumph, riding right into your face.

It Spoke of Exactly the Things

You stumble drunk from Alabama to Abalone Cove, facing Catalina.

Okay. Abalone Cove. What is it?

Sea lilies, gulls over the rock eddies, wind-humming flute holes in the rocks that are drunk hags with time, their flutes . . .

No are not, liar. Remember they are just it, themselves. You spent half your life getting apt poetry into women who were not it. They were very little, in fact. You never loved but too much, into the dream. You get some nagging bride of the dollar and new wallpaper, clap a miracle around her.

Hell, your last woman couldn't even *appear* without a tribe of witnesses. All she wanted was a pillow stuffed with old hat. She and her grown kids like to sniff around beauty and grace, not touching it, like scared hyenas.

They held to sanity so hard they were insane.

Where you say eat or be eaten.

Driven out of the stinking chicken South by

ghouls lousy with self-regard. All this nimble jabber to the point that you are scaring us shitless, good folks not worthy of shoveling Shakespeare's house of night soil. The halls of the college stank with the corpses of every inconsequential fool who'd had his way with drying up the day. The university was a neo-Grecian dump with a good ball team. The only thing was to get drunk and fire at will. The chairman fired back with drinking and eating female students.

Ah, those beauties sweet to me when I was down: Val, Ann, Rita Veranoff, a few others who can't be told because of their boyfriends.

To San Pedro, on the peninsula south of Los Angeles.

What's this, windsurfing—board with sail?

At Cabrillo Beach, a nigger beach, says my South African sea-captain friend Basil, they have these things. They run out fast, very fast, keeling over, a fast lean ripping out, against the surf. It was a noble thing, with the danger required. I once saw a man out beyond the farthest buoy, a mile and a half out or so. That would do. The boats from Ports of Call came close. I even saw one boy climb from his board onto a pleasure boat and they went off with him.

I was at the Twenty-second Street landing, listening to the pilots talk. There was a girl with a turquoise ring. She had found a dog, a Siberian, running free. She had him on a piece of rope and he was under the table where they were drinking beer. The pilots were punk. One, like a heavy graduate student, sucked on a curved pipe. He kept repeating the word *unnecessary*.

There was much on the job that was unnecessary. He wore socks with rubber shower shoes over them, black socks. He was at his leisure. Before I left, I looked at the girl. They said she could pilot as well as any of them. I believe it. She said little and was an image, a real California image. You could not get it better.

The man told me about the tidal wave of 1959. It came in over the breakwater and lifted everything in sight. He also told me there used to be fish in the Pacific Ocean. There were once living people in San Pedro also. Sometimes a man on a hang glider will go off the cliffs of Paseo del Mar. He will crash, break himself up, and then the lifeguard and ambulance drivers will come. The ambulance drivers like to save Negroes and then mutter about cutting their heads off. I was friends with one of those ambulance drivers who liked me until I got on my feet. When I got on my feet, I told him I wasn't taking any more.

California is an excellent place for polishing your hatreds. The countryside is gorgeous and has made all the Californianas into morons. They all deserve a drunken, abusive stepfather, like I was. They call for the mirror always. Ah, well, what you cannot correct you can at least insult. They need plenty of rest and expensive food and constant petting. It requires high health to murder the day with banality. Mom bathes a lot. The odor of cradlepuke from grown children must get dire at times.

When the whaleboats were in dock, I went down and asked one of the captains for some whaleshit. They sell it for fertilizer. He argued a while, but I came back up Nineteenth Street with a bag. Then I went down to the pawnshop and I traded in a motorcycle helmet and fifty dollars. The Mexicans moved off as I went out to Cabrillo with the whaleshit and the piece. I had my landlady's hacksaw and in the garage I cut the thing down.

I knew when the two of them were leaving because I had been there when the mother booked the boat at Ports of Call. I knew the tour the captain would give them because he was one of those feckless whiners at the Twenty-second Street landing. She was giving the son a ride because he had at last graduated from college. You saw them driving around town together. The mother was a looker. She was the small-breasted type with long legs that I found inductive. You saw them at the YMCA, jogging together, and at the Moroccan restaurant, tearing bread together. I saw her first coming out of Mary Star Church, with the boy, of course. The boy had on a coat and was very set on himself. He was the apple of his mother's eye. She, no doubt, had a pet name for him and doted on his cowish eyes. I am good for faces. He had the complacent air of the petted one, the user, the incubated, the bloodsucker, the gigolo of his mother's blind affection. He would be the kind requiring constant assurances from her, constant denials of his meritlessness. He would have droll truisms aplenty for her. There was something nasty and sly about their collusion. Well I knew, well I knew. Forever she would mistake this simpering pig for a stallion, her royal boy. He would exploit her foolish, helpless matronage from now till dust.

. . .

I saw him at the Moroccan restaurant and knew all this almost instantly. What a slick puppy in the lap of grace he was. Their jokes were repulsive, a sort of baby talk. He would mumble, she would treasure. She cast hallowed glances toward him.

Otherwise, she was lovely.

When he left for the rest room, the woman looked at me.

I was frankly wanting her.

There were sidelong looks toward me throughout the rest of the dinner. She was not displeased. The boy caught on and then hastened away, deliberately ignoring me.

I laughed.

But I was lonely, angry, and my need was deep.

It chanced I saw her at the window in Ports of Call, near Errol Flynn's old yacht in the berth. She wanted to go sailing to San Francisco, she and the boy. The boat she hired was cedar decked, grand. She had to be wealthy. The sun was around her shoulders and her lean balsa-colored arms. I wanted her very much. Her hair was rare—loose heaped curls of auburn. Between her breasts, in the slit of her blouse, was a curious thing—a tiny black tattooed butterfly.

This brought a sweat on me.

It spoke of exactly the things.

It gave hope.

On Sunday morning I saw the cedarwood boat

tacking out of the harbor. The two of them were holding each other like lovers in the bow, as people do early in the trip. My vest was on, rather cumbersome as it was, and I mounted the board. The wind was brisk and I was off.

The speed of the Windsurfer is shocking. You get a pleasant riot of nerves in the lower stomach, something very elastic, as from your first high drop in a swing.

Flashing against the surf you go, leaping six feet above the whitecaps and pushing the mast aright to squirm flat into the chop, wind crying to your ears. You are close to spilling gism into your shorts, a helpless twisting and slipping, full rapid joy. Eventually, the water is slate, like a rooftop spilling and parting around you. The sun was just peeking in the gray around Catalina. The metal next to my chest gave me some tiny discomfort.

A mile out or so I came on them, a hundred yards from the buoy. I neared the brown craft. It was a splendid, sculpted, headlong thing, thrusting ahead with no mind to me, and I felt diminished. I might never see the woman again. Such is the population of California that often you never see someone again. I sensed the absurd smallness of myself, my petty desires, my murky ratlike aggression.

I hit the yacht and fell over.

I could hear their cries of alarm and I rested in the water. They turned, sails down, motoring back to me, and the face of the boy appeared at the bow.

He was looking at me, very smug, all the condescension of an ambulance driver.

"You need help?"

He was humorous.

I brought the sawed-off gun out of my vest and fired it, both barrels. The gun went off a little under the surface of the water, and spouts flew out over him with the whaleshit, which almost entirely blackened him, body and face.

He was in white. He tore at his eyes. I dropped the gun, and it fled from me in the water. Then I righted the board and was away as they were still shouting.

Back to Cabrillo Beach.

I never saw the progress of the cedarwood boat.

I was desolate for days afterward. Though I don't drink anymore, I went to Peppy's bar on Ninth Street and acted out the melancholy of the drunk—questioning my worth, reckoning whether I was heroic truly or merely possessed of a dangerous spite. I threatened the bartender's life and left.

I was very despondent. San Pedro was a black bright town of no succor, and I was weary of the chattering Mexicans, their blasted loud race. On the radios they would not quit the duets denying their constant failure, their atonal search for the right hubcap.

At the Moroccan restaurant, I was eating, and her waist—she was in shorts, sandals, a batik shirt—appeared next to my iced tea. She was looking down at me strangely. There was a passion in her eyes.

"Did you go to San Francisco?" I asked.

"No."

"Where's your son?"

"I don't know. He's grown."

"Do you like my new blond hair?"

"I knew you, anyway."

"Would you like me to drive my tongue into your vagina?"

"Yes."

I brought her back South with me. She liked to give me money, and she could get plenty of drugs. She had some kind of perpetual, rather harmless disease that entitles her to a drug.

They had invited me to speak at Biloxi. I began my speech.

"Liars! Masquerados! Doomed pretenders!"

They loved it, shivering in ecstasy, as did she. The check was slipped to me by grateful alarmed hands. They were next to swooning with fear of me.

Later, the two of us were out in the thunderstorm, a lightning run of astonishing proportions, the boat rocking, creaking. Lightning ran out above us with a calamitous distress. Thunder wracked the waves.

I supported myself spread legged on the deck. In the light from the lightning we injected the drug together. With one hand in her hair and the other around a flare pistol, I shouted yes! yes! yes! in the rain. She kneeled and sucked wolfishly at me, tossed away from my stomach but returning again and again. Once she fell away and bruised her cheek on the gunwale but returned with frantic surrender, a choked cry of love in her throat. I fired the flare—again, again, shouting into the thunder, drenched like a monument by the rain. The lightning ripped open the night, and I watched with wide eyes the black butterfly pumping between her breasts.

Bold as love, bold as love!

So, in Abalone Cove, where the water washes in full of the rust from old wrecks, the rust from my sunken shotgun washing over her tanned feet, I sit, still stunned by carnivorous passion when the drug runs out.

I drank enough.

I banged the walls of space and time long enough. I don't have to lie. I think of the black butterfly and sometimes I can even remember her name.

Fans

Wright's father, a sportswriter and a hack and a shill for the university team, was sitting next to Milton, who was actually blind but nevertheless a rabid fan, and Loomis Orange, the dwarf who was one of the team's managers. The bar was out of their brand of beer, and they were a little drunk, though they had come to that hard place together where there seemed nothing, absolutely nothing to say.

The waitress was young. Normally, they would have commented on her and gone on to pursue the topic of women, the perils of booze, or the like. But not now. Of course it was the morning of the big game in Oxford, Mississippi.

Someone opened the door of the bar, and you could see the bright wonderful football morning pouring in with the green trees, the Greek-front buildings, and the yelling frat boys. Wright's father and Loomis Orange looked up and saw the morning. Loomis Orange smiled, as did Milton, hearing the shouts of the college men. The father did not smile. His son had come in the door, swaying and rolling, with one hand to his chest and his walking stick in the other.

Wright's father turned to Loomis and said, "Loomis, you are an ugly distorted little toad."

Loomis dropped his glass of beer.

"*What?*" the dwarf said.

"I said that you are ugly," Wright said.

"How could you have said that?" Milton broke in.

Wright's father said, "Aw, shut up, Milton. You're just as ugly as he is."

"What've I ever did to you?" cried Milton.

Wright's father said, "Leave me alone! I'm a writer."

"You ain't any kind of writer. You an alcoholic. And your wife is ugly. She's so skinny she almost ain't even there!" shouted the dwarf.

People in the bar—seven or eight—looked over as the three men spread, preparing to fight. Wright hesitated at a far table, not comprehending.

His father was standing up.

"Don't, don't, don't," Wright said. He swayed over toward their table, hitting the floor with his stick, moving tables aside.

The waitress shouted over, "I'm calling the cops!"

Wright pleaded with her: "Don't, don't, don't!"

"Now, please, sit down everybody!" somebody said.

They sat down. Wright's father looked with hatred at Loomis. Milton was trembling. Wright made his way slowly over to them. The small bar crowd settled back to their drinks and conversation on the weather, the game, traffic, etc. Many of the people talked about J. Edward Toole, whom all of them called simply Jet. The name went with him. He was in the Ole Miss defensive secondary, a handsome figure who was everywhere on the field, the star of the team.

Wright found a seat at the table. He could half see and he looked calmly at all of them. His voice was extremely soft, almost ladylike, very Southern. Wright was born again, just like Jet, who led the team in prayer before every game.

"Let's talk about Jet. I know him well," Wright began.

His father shifted, embarrassed. "We know that, Son."

"I grew up with that boy," he went on.

"Wright, we know. . . ."

"We shared the normal boyhood things together. We were little strangers on this earth together. We gamboled in the young pastures. We took our first forbidden pleasures together"—he winked—"our first cigarette, our first beer." Wright paused, shyly. "I shared my poetry with him."

"God," said Wright's father.

"We met when he and the other boys chased me down the beach with air rifles, shooting me repeatedly on my bare back, legs, and ears until they had run me to earth. He was always large and swift. He used to pinch me in the hall and pull out my tee shirt so that it looked as if I had breasts. He used to flatulate in his desk and point at me. In point of the fair sex, there was always a gag from this merry lad. He took my poems and revised them into pornographic verse, complete with sketches, mind you, and sent them to my sweetheart—"

"Son," pleaded Wright's father.

"Oh, I even tried the field with him myself, though thin of leg. He was a champion already, only a sophomore at Bay High. I will say that he, ha ha, taught me very well how to fumble on return of punts and kickoffs. For such was I used—as swift fodder for the others."

Loomis and Milton were entranced. Wright's father was breathing very heavy and looking at the floor.

"*Wright.*" This time he was almost demanding.

"Those smashes of his! I certainly, ha ha, coughed up the ball and often limped into the showers. One afternoon while no one was looking, he clipped me from behind, right on the concrete floor."

Wright was smiling meekly as his voice trailed off. And when he went on, it was quieter but very even.

"We won all the games. I say we, though I stood on the sidelines or played in the band—French horn. I remember his beautiful mother watching from the stands, but what I mainly remember was Jet, with all his tackles and interceptions. He was All-State his junior year, then went on to duplicate that his senior, ultimately receiving, as you know, a full scholarship to the university here, where fate—or most likely God —brought my family and me to this fair city, my father finding employment and I a convenient although irregular education."

Wright's father's hands were over his face.

"It's back to the night of our senior graduation from Bay High, that night you are familiar with—"

"Yes, God damn it, we are familiar!" said his father.

"Wait. I want to hear the story again," said Loomis Orange.

"Yeah. Again," said Milton.

"That night, knowing I had my new Vespa motor scooter as a present from father and mother, Jet and some of the boys waited at the end of the driveout from the auditorium. Still wearing my robe, my mortarboard under my arm, I cranked up that lovely red Vespa for all it could rip. I was in a hurry to change and join Jet and the others out at the lake party. They were in the bushes on either side of the road with a rope lying hidden between them. Well, they 'clotheslined' me. The rest is history."

"Yes, Son! We *know* about that and your condition, bless your heart. Let's—"

Wright's father rose as if to go.

"Then . . ."

"*Then?*" said Loomis. He put his short arms on the table. He wore a bulky child's size Izod shirt.

"*Then? Then?*" said the father. He sat back down.

"The best, I suppose, in a way, ha ha. At the end of the summer, when I was out of the hospital and all was said and done, Jet and I made a private trip to the Biloxi Yacht Club. We were interested in a boat. Or rather, as I usually did, I followed his interests. It was late in the afternoon and there had been a bumper crop of shrimp—so many they were falling off the boat. The sharks had followed the boats in and they'd called off swimming.

"A man on the dock was balling up hamburger meat full of razor blades, in chunks about the size of horse apples, and throwing them in the water. The water would churn and a fan of blood would rush out of the shark's head. This brought the others to it. The water was white and thrashing. Heads and half bodies floated up and snapped back down. Then the alligator gars got into it and it was bleeding paradise. That was Jet's phrase. Oh, he could do the smart phrase now and then, using a British term or some such.

"It was *bleeding paradise*, he said. After he finished saying this over and over again, he asked me what I thought. Thought about *what?* I said. And Jet got very sad and looked out over the water at the red sun. Then he pushed me in."

"He pushed you *in?* In the *water?*" said Milton, who was the only one at the table who could respond in words.

"Yes," said Wright. There was a bit of hurt in his eyes, but they retained an even, soft gleam. "But there is the further beautiful thing."

"He pushed you in the water, Son?"

"Yes. But last year I saw him on campus. I knew that he'd been born again and I wanted to congratulate him. You know what he said to me as he rubbed that big Sugar Bowl ring on those great sunbrowned fingers of his? He put his arm on my shoulder and said to me, 'Wright, I'm sorry.'"

There was business to do, the game to see, or feel, so the four of them slowly left the bar, tapping, wobbling, huffing, and met Wright's mother on the corner, then went up to the stadium to wait for Jet to kill them.

Power and Light

[AN IDEA FOR FILM]

Citizens,

These are the Cascades, high-strutting and holy in the dawn. A chorus from Tchaikovsky sings the morning. The water of the mountain gathers, rolls, and pours, an echoing white churning brute, over the fall. White blood of the land. A gray glorious pulpit of rocks. Washington state, most watered.

This solitariness does not need the jet. But the plane, a tiny sporting emblem, comes from afar and dips down into the face of the fall, twists out and rises, this F-14 Tomcat, frolics up, rolling through a heavy gray air.

In Puget Sound, the shipyards nearby, the men in the boat are well drunk. They've been fishing all night and Olympia beer cans litter the deck of the sixteen-footer. One of the men is strained from looking. He has an odd fixed grimace.

"Boys, boys. It's just too much water's what it is. Too much."

The others groan.

"Was settled by snards. Named for a peaceable Indian."

The man looks around like a coy detective.

"We got any peaceable Indians?"

The drunkest of all, an Indian in a filthy flannel shirt, is plucked up by two mates. He smiles, though almost catatonic, his black teeth gaping.

They drop him. The men mumble randomly.

"A mother and daughter at the same time?"

"Where?"

"Swonderful. 'Oh, what a vision of ecstasy! Her knees on the floor, her arse to me!' "

"Where?"

Little Willy, a blind boy in a high silver Stetson hat, plays his harmonica on a Seattle street. He misses a lick, says "Doo doo!"

The tiny afflicted brat continues.

High on a light pole, a rolling almost cumulus of fog around, a workman in a hard hat twists back and forth at a connection. The light pole is atop a tall building. The men on the roof lift their faces. Something is crucial.

Ladies and Gentlemen,
Polly Buck steps on the porch of her large duplex,

boots on, carrying her helmet, lunch pail. The gray Seattle sky lies around her, filmy and thick, like you could eat it.

Melton is sitting on the porch his side of the duplex, not saying a word but looking at her too frozenly. They might not be on speaking terms anymore, because she gives a weary smirk as she opens the door. Melton emits a queer buzzing sound. Maybe he's a little angry. This girl has done nothing for him.

High on the light pole behind them, the hard-hatted workman twists, jerks. Something is refractory.

The hands of a man in a hotel room are brown and handsome and they rest on brown vellum paper, in the right hand a fountain pen. The envelope into which the note is folded is brown too. But the script is large, looping, and unpracticed. There is a pair of binoculars on the desk. And there is a roll of stamps with a fierce beaked eagle on them. "Organized Labor Proud and Free" is imprinted.

Through the window, high up, the workman bangs with an implement.

Polly Buck has a roommate, Larry Lynn Idol, sitting on the couch in a big tent dress. Polly gets down to her bra. It's dirty at the edges, not too sexy. She collects the mail from a table. There is a brown envelope. On it is the big looping curious script.

Through a binocular's view: The workman twists, writhes. Just a minute. Some hair falls out. It's a woman. The fog pours past and covers the gazing men around the bottom of the light pole.

A man in a three-piece suit, hail fellow well met, black hair parted in the middle, walks with a glorious white bulldog, spiked superb collar, down another Seattle street. He stops at a kiosk where a whiskered old hippie sells him the newsrag *High Society* and mints. He walks. Peers into a restaurant. People are eating enormous crabs—butter, lettuce falling from their lips. The bulldog rushes for the open door. The thin, big-breasted receptionist says to the man,

"He can't."

"I know," says the man. "He can do other things," the man says. "His dog things."

The man smiles. This citizen might be a Princeton graduate. He has nice shoes, a nice tie. But he has a wet, now wetter mouth, full liverish lips.

There is a dictionary on the table in the room where the handsome brown fingers are—circling words. He, whoever, is very carefully circling quite ordinary words.

Ladies and Gentlemen,

Polly Buck takes the brown note from the brown envelope. There is a piano in the bare room, a rail for ballet, a single tall chrome lamp, no rug. Larry Lynn, in her vast moomoo dress, has never risen from the maroon leather couch. This large duplex is spare, arty.

Larry Lynn has wet eyes. Polly is turned from her, reading the note. It reads,

> *You have an appointment with something large. Don't be late. God keep you.*
>   *Sweed Truitt*

"I don't like this," says Polly.

"What is it?" asks Larry Lynn.

Polly shoves the note at her.

Larry Lynn scans it, hands it back. It has not made much impression.

"I don't know any Sweed Truitt," says Polly.

Polly turns to see Larry Lynn whole for the first time. There is a lot of her. Larry Lynn might be on the verge of tears.

"What's wrong?" Polly regards her own dirty fingers. "You didn't go to work again."

"Polly."

"What? What is it, Lare?"

"I have a lump. I'm sure I have a lump."

"Where?"

"My breast. Where, where, where," she mocks the world and Polly.

Larry Lynn peers up warmly. She gathers her moomoo hem a little with her ring-fingered hand. She is a sitting open bucket of nerve matter. There's a big dramatic mouth on her.

The workman on the pole is limp from her efforts. Then she begins writhing and yanking again, like a doll on strings.

. . .

Here is yet another woman, Ruth, in a kitchenette, near the sink. What's happening with this woman? She's a slick blond knockout of a woman, but she's heaving at the sink. Outside the fog rolls past in gouts, rushing wisps over a berry field.

Ahh, ah, Ruth pants. Her hands are placed on the counter. There is a slim white man far behind her in the living room. He cannot see, but he can hear her as he watches the basketball game on television, and he turns his face—sort of a lightweight, fair-haired type, this man.

There are Dilantin pills, the bottle turned over, on the counter beyond Ruth's fingers.

"Ruth?" calls the man.

"It's all right. I choked. I don't need anything."

"What!?"

"Nothing."

The man moves in the background. Ruth grabs the pills, crams them in the bottle. This is a secret, a big one.

On a hook on the kitchen wall is a Navy coat, officer's hat with filigree. Somebody here is a pilot.

Ruth is coming back, looking morbidly at the running gusts of fog. Her eyes are running too. She imagines, imagines. The strong woman has been left limp by the onslaught. Her eyes race up into the thick gray and the antennae of a tenement building. Something about her is very willful, dreaming tough, harassed dreams of power. The Dilantin bottle shatters in her hands. This is a tough beauty, Ruth.

The man is suddenly at her back, grinning. She hears but won't turn around.

"Hey. When you going to teach me to fly?" he says.

He eats at an apple effetely, yellowish boots on him. Perhaps he is a professor of theater somewhere, since he has a cultured, practiced voice.

He's light haired like she is. He seems an odd choice of man for her. Her eyes narrow, get narrower and narrower. She sees something on the building top.

"Look, Ian. On top of that building."

Fleasize, at the cross of the pole, in the tumbling fog—closer, closer—it's the hard-hat electrician, struggling. No face can be seen, but the hair is long, and the woman's bottom in jeans is very interesting, twisting. She loses footing, scrambles, flails inside her belt.

The lights around Ruth and Ian go out.

The apartment is dark.

Then it relights.

At the T of the pole on the top of the building a tool is dropped. The body hangs limp, helmet tumbling down, long hair tumbling, waving in fog blasts.

Like dead.

The body shudders.

"It's a woman," says Ian.

"Yes. A sister," says Ruth.

Next door to Angel St. James's house is Fritz Walls's. You can see him sweeping his patio now. He looks to be a basketball player about two decades out of training. He has a pronounced belly, white high-top sneakers, beer jowls, a light ash of whiskers.

It's morning, early.

Looking pleasantly dead, Angel St. James, forty-ish, does not wake immediately to the blast from her digital clock radio. Then, sweet Lord, she *is* awake. Nobody is this happy to wake up, but this straw-haired dispatcher for City Lights is. She's nuts about the morning. She jumps up, making bop bop didoodlee oop, bop dibi di bop sounds, drumming on her thigh. Di bop di bop. Loony with morning light as Fritz Walls sweeps his patio across from the window. This female is not on any happiness-with-job chart. She goes off the line. Nobody would have credence. She's on the bed making like a maid on amphetamines. Now she's perking in the kitchen. There are beer cans everywhere, but she's got a system that mows them down. She moves them all down the counter and into a popped-out grocery sack—pow!—with a snap of her wrist, and trots them into the garbage pail. Next to the can outdoors.

Fritz Walls nods.

She nods.

Maybe they've once said hello.

He gathers the hose, but he hates it. He hates his wristwatch when he looks at it, despises the cigarette he's lighting. He coughs out the night with the noise of a rake over iron—haaack!

Bop didi bop.

We notice somebody else in Angel's house now that she's noised around, pitching eggs in the air. Somebody is shaking the floor in the back of the house. It's her own house, but it's not that solid. Then again it's hers.

Wait. There's something curious in the little dining room. It's an ant farm, a whole civilization—queen, workers dithering in their tunnels. She gives a pause and watches them fiddle around through the glass panes.

The person lumbering about in the back room is Robbie, her son. Angel keeps up the bop didi bidi bop, slapping on her thighs. Robbie is not too pleased by the morning. He scrapes his crotch with long hairy fingers, is stricken by a long obscene canine yawn, tongue licking about. This man is an oaf in the employ of Boeing. At Boeing he is a security guard. A diploma from Security College is the only thing on his wall. He looks into the mirror, into the long rut of nothing. It is with sick fear that he gazes at himself as he tugs on his uniform shirt, his tie. He has gruesome black utility shoes on white thin legs. He has sick fear and passionate love for himself.

His mother, Angel, hovers at the door.

He seems to be ill, sneering at the kitchen odors, finger in his nose. He puts on his pants over the shoes, stumbles.

In the dining room, he stares with loathing at the ant farm on the counter of the sideboard. He studies the ants while Angel finishes the eggs and sausages in the kitchen. He works his fingers back and forth like a pianist, imitating their legs. Spying the queen bee, Robbie makes humping motions with his hips at her. The drone sycophants are around her. He takes earwax from his ear and smears it on the glass pane.

"Hey, boys," Robbie says to the workers, "it's

Miller time," and then he goes back to his room for his gun belt and pocket watch.

His hat is in his hand; his hair is wet from combing. Robbie has a nervous tic, rather constantly brushing his hair back. He takes the pistol out of its holster, puts the gun belt down, begins removing cartridges from it.

Angel has been decreasingly humming the bibop di bi bop, di bidi bop boo, slapping her thighs a little less; shining, smiling, a little less.

She watches Robbie slowly load the revolver.

When he leaves, she gazes at the ant farm. Then she goes to a stack of papers and mail in her bedroom. On top of the stack is an opened brown envelope. Her eyes are worried about this. Then she reaches into a slot of her bed table. The picture of her ex-husband is curled. There is an X penned across his face.

He's not bad-looking: swarthy, smiling, lusty.

She works on the pen marks a little with her fingernail.

She lifts her breasts with both hands and wiggles like a stripper writhing at the prospect of the day, then runs for the shower.

The man with the glorious white bulldog is watching the front of Polly Buck's duplex as she and the large Larry Lynn emerge wearing tennis shoes and boating sports clothes. Melton sits on his porch and eyes them venomously. When they are gone up the street, the man steps to the curb, then daintily across the street to Melton's walk. Melton is wearing an ear-stud and a turned-down sailor's cap. He's playing with a cracked golf ball, unwinding the endless rubber strands.

"Is that a Miss Polly Buck?" asks the man with the dog.

"You let that thing come near me, I'll stomp its head," Melton says.

"Yes. He's not. This leash is strong. And I am strong," the man says.

"You be dragging flat fur down the road," Melton says.

"Yes. Miss Polly Buck," the man says.

"Be a got damn rug on a chain," Melton says.

"Surely. But Miss Buck," the man says and comes a step closer. "Miss Buck," the man in the suit, center-parted hair, says, drawing up his liverish lips, keening eyes, bewildered.

Melton is insane, a casualty of a long impossible lust.

"She works on the wires, doesn't she?" the man with the bulldog asks.

"Yes, wires, wires," Melton says. "That's right, wires."

"Quite a spokesman you are," the man says. "So tell me, what's Miss Buck like?"

"Twat on wheels," Melton says.

The bulldog moves to lick Melton.

"Hi, flat dog," Melton says.

The man leashes the dog away.

"Woman make a man lick like a dog. Break your heart, walk over it; ain't no light down there. It's always going to be there. But Jesus, never," Melton says.

"No," says the man. "Is there anything particular about her?"

"Yeah."

But Melton won't say.

"What, my man. What?"

"Unnaturalism. With the fat one with her."

Melton raises a cupped hand to the place above his lips.

"Uh," says the bulldog man.

He toils away. The liverish lips are at work, pursing.

Aeroscan of birds, all kinds of seabirds, sea, Puget Sound with boat life, wharfs, seals, howling noisy seabirds again, here and there a helicopter. We penetrate the special leaden weather, down with the wharfside rummies in the Cold Crab café. A bearded woman in a bright flowered wrap sits sucking coffee. Her hair is bleached a vile startling blond. She is still on the make but forgets the goat wisps of gray and white around her lips. Sitting beside her is an old Mexican hooker, long greasy hair barretted, a flower at her temple; a shuffling, still-endeavoring woman. This woman is really not that old.

Around, down, up. Deformations or rude beauties. Decayed-tooth Indians grinning in the back of a pickup truck. A tattooed man running down the street pursued by a cop. There is a crying woman in front of a department store.

.   .   .

Night.

We see in the emergency room of a great hospital, we see the officious confusion that attends the staff in this mournful ward.

An injured power worker, a man, holds his bloody head. His bud commiserates.

"Only a cunt. It had to be a cunt. I leave a screaming cunt at home and then a cunt drops her hat on me. She slips. Nothing wrong with her. Naw. Nothing wrong with *her*."

The man with the brown handsome hands is stepping around the hotel room slowly. He stops and pronounces a word:

"*Time. Time. Time.*"

There is a word underlined in the *t*s of the dictionary on his desk. "Time," he pronounces again slowly. He is agitated. The pages of the dictionary whirl before him. He upsets the binoculars. Then he pauses a while.

"*Happen. Happen.*" He turns the pages.

Happen is underlined heavily. The sheets of brown paper are neatly stacked. There is absolutely no sound when he is not pronouncing the words. The man is deaf and there is something archaic, a bit ingenuous to his mien.

He goes to a page where other words are written, their definitions copied out in the big loose script. The page trembles.

"Woman." He pauses a long while. "*Up* woman." He reflects. "No. *High woman.*"

No other sound is heard. Only the wires outside his window are contiguous with other life.

. . .

A solitary black woman is in an enormous cathedral, a skyscraping gaudy one. She is moving her lips and her eyes are distressed. The cathedral is dark. A baroque gloom filters through the nave from the windows. The statuary and iconography lean toward the tortured, the agonized. The Virgin doesn't look too happy and the Child looks positively doubtful.

The black woman doesn't cross herself. Cathedral music of mournful, even sinister, rumination comes on. Her feet in black heels click out the aisle, out to the portico—still swift and clicking—onto the walk and running wind, rolling leaves, big spattered leaves as if the sky is shedding. The tree trunks around her have the paralyzed gestures of horrid bodies, passions. Flickering on her face is resolve, then a miserable pout, then a big-eyed what? Fear.

She walks a considerable distance through a block of dingy brownstones. A garbage can lid falls off its can as if spontaneously, revealing a Negro doll whole, perfect. But wait, there is an enormous wharf rat with the doll's wrist in its teeth. The rat has knocked the lid off the can. This is a rough and nasty region. There is hardly a light around the neighborhood. A door is open but there is no activity in the foyer.

Now the black woman walks up the steps of a nicer entrance. The wainscoting is white and clean. She has the key in her hand. In the mailbox, among the few white envelopes is a brown one. All is straight in the orangeish mellow light of the lobby. The wall art is notable: pictures of solemn Zambesi women and men lurk profoundly. They have the fine austere carriage of the warrior class.

But the library, small as it is, is trashed. There are books thrown everywhere. The lamp is down. In the breakfast room there lies about her a sloppy riot of dishes, overturned coffee, smashed oranges. Somebody has taken a newspaper apart page by page and littered the kitchen. Pages continue into the black foreboding slot of the hall. Her feet follow them—sports, want ads, headlines. The walk is very difficult for her. There is not a sound. And at the end—dry clicking music comes on—though she raps at the door, the lack of reply is deep and almost resonant.

The black woman eases the door in.

It's a shambles—a wreckage of upset chair, phone off the hook, cast-off garments, broken cigarette packs, butts and spilled ashtray on the leopard throw rug. A dark blue blanket is humped on the bed. It arises.

Here is a horror: Lou.

We have seen junkies before, but this is an order of new.

Lou is emaciated, a stick man, like a starving child in the ads. His underpants are yellowed. He wears heavy mascara and stripes, leonine war paint but badly drawn. His eyes are wide and sick. His voice is loud, like that of a cerebral palsy victim.

"Aloo!"

He grins and the teeth are bloody and dreadful, the gums white.

The black woman does cross herself now. She's frozen, terrified.

Lou hisses.

"You wasn't Catholic in Mississippi." Drool comes from his white gums.

"Lou!" She trembles.

Lou pulls up a magnifying glass—this skeleton man, his legs a dead gray. The arms are mottled with tracks.

"And still a virgin. A *weregin*," he says, as in trembling German burgher talk. "Rabbit meat!"

Now we see a birdcage is open, and the loose parrot squawks from the curtains, flails across the room, terrified. The black woman's arms rise. She's stunned, eyes shut. Feathers fall around the wild-loaded Lou.

The odor must be something raw. Parrot droppings are here and there on the furnishings. But on the vanity counter, very cleanly kept, are Lou's fixings: neatly bagged heroin and cocaine, a tie-off tube, a hypo. The black woman's nostrils are offended.

"Oh, Lou," she can barely say it. "Honey."

Maureen reaches down for a page of the newspaper but surrenders it back to the floor, hopeless. She walks back to the front of the place.

In the forward room she looks at the telephone. Tears rim her eyes. An ambulance right out in the street shrieks by, close, as if it's coming to the door, then passes.

On a notebook dumped among the spilled books of the sitting room, she reads some barely legible scrawl. She lays the book down, begins collecting the rest strewn about the floor. Then she picks out the brown envelope from the stack of mail and holds it, does not open it yet. Other things are with her.

There is a mirror in the room, into which the

black woman now peers. It reveals a fatigued, tender woman—long-suffering eyes. She looks confusedly at the telephone. Then she takes her jacket and goes to the door. Her shoes click on the steps, and right in front of her at the bottom step is the glorious white bulldog.

It doesn't like Negroes, lifts up a lip and growls.

It is towed back on the leash.

The man looks at her—long and unblinking, no apologies.

She's very nervous. She slowly moves, then whisks off down the walk, the man watching her.

Behold the isolated walrus on a rock island!

What is a walrus, what in hell is a walrus, anyway?

From front-on of its face, whiskers, we see the eternal furry mourning of the walrus. These sea eyes are deep and we study them like subatomics. The walrus is the powerful sloth of lust. The sea cow is on another rock. What is a sea cow? How does it go for the sea cow? We range in and see the almost horrible perplexed creation of mammal and fish together. The mother is waddling for fish, off then nimble in the cold dark impossible water. The walrus guards the whole absurdity. He is so great and so expendable. So on with camera philosophy.

Man, it is wet here and heavy in the air and it's hard to fly, yak the seabirds.

Comes a churning boat past, riding the rolling gray with much smoke behind. It is a sixteen-footer, with Polly Buck at the helm. Larry Lynn, the fat one, is terrified in a corner of the boat, sternward. Holding her ears, she shakes amply. What a wet noisy hell. Her tent dress is all spotted with wet.

This boat is Polly Buck's, by damn. She's seized it with her new loot on the job, and though it moves along with great poot and smoke, it is the living end. Unmindful of the shaken and fretting Larry Lynn, Polly Buck's really *piloting* this thing, really the captain.

The weather, the choppy iron sea are not right at all for this excursion.

There's nobody else in the large gray helisphere, and with a zeppelin's eye we see the boat lonely, making its forward streaks in the water, the fierce and blown-haired tiny captain making for the smug horizon.

Ladies and gentlemen,
Polly Buck amidst her work.

The wires are enormous, colored bold blues, oranges, purples, yellows!

Fog rises as if the electricity is leaking out of the wires, and any fool knows that enormous electrical power and water like this do not mix without imminent death. We expect to see a frizzing, smoked girl shortly. But she hoists, fits the strand, wipes her brow. Her helmet may be seen as that of a true warrior for power and light—legislating it, regulating it, as if from the deeps.

Men around her are a blur.

Some of the things she lifts are really too big for her, but up they go.

This girl is chaining your breakfast together, citizen. She is hitching the light up for your asinine patio party, your old starlight teevee movies, your electric toothbrush, vibrator, Magic Fingers.

Then we beam on a colossal lightworks—an atomic plant, a dam—lines stretching across mammoth struts, Ts, figures of massive artwork in the gray sky. The Olympic and Cascade ranges spread with heavy cables running through this natural paradise. Mount Rainier rises. All is heavy with water power. State of Washington—the most electrified state of the United States—Seattle, builder of ships.

Lake Washington stretches.

Water, water, water.

Male figures come into focus. Sweat runs heavy from Polly.

Two men watch through a glass. One smiles sheepishly at the other, watching the trim Polly bend to her work.

She removes her helmet and throws out her pretty wet hair. She catches the looks of the men. She smiles, just a frank, mutually felicitous smile. The man with the coffee returns it with a wink. Brothers and sisters on the job.

Then they are drinking beer together at a tavern. Nobody defers to Polly. She's just one of the guys in their favorite haunt. She really is at home here. Sand-slide bowling goes on among rednecks, unemployed cowboys, Orientals, Indians, under the broken Budweiser clock. In its light Polly catches change in the air and buys a round. The jukebox is active—Johnny

Paycheck. A drunk argues about the time. The married man can't take his eyes off Polly. His look is benign, fatherly. Polly is happily tired. She puts her head on her crossed arms on the table.

"Polly?" he asks gently.

"Uh?"

"You all right?"

"Sure. Tired."

"Hey. You were good."

"Good?"

"Yeh. Just real good."

"Oh, well. Thanks." She really doesn't know what to do with the compliment.

"Something big is going to happen to you. I feel it."

"Something big?" She's confused, then angry. "Lookit. You don't write letters, do you?"

"Letters?" He's surprised by her anger. "I meant something nice, real nice, is bound to happen to you."

She gets a sudden elbow, no apology, from a careless worker next to her.

"Hey, Polly," says somebody else. "You know why niggers stink?"

"So blind people can hate them too," she fires back.

It's an old one.

An iron-haired man with a cane enters the bar; he's in his sixties, a perilous solicitude to his manner and searching eyes.

"Ah, horseshit," says the careless worker.

"What? Huh?" The whole table turns to look.

"It's Hospital Hank. Get low. Ah, shit."

Hospital Hank has found them.

"Somebody fake a hernia. Show him your head, Cecil," the careless worker whispers to the injured worker at the end of the table.

"Who is this?" asks Polly.

"It's—" begins the married man. But Hank is too close.

"Gentlemen, gentlemen." Hank notices Polly, tries to rephrase, can't, smiles pleasantly, and draws up a chair.

Hank zeroes in on the fellow with the bandaged head. The married man draws closer to Polly as Hank starts a violently sympathetic monologue, barely heard, with the bandaged man.

"Back in the forties, there was a disaster on the Cascade Crossover. They just call it the Calamity now, anybody that remembers. There was an overrun, some beams went down, and seven—"

"Six," interrupts the careless worker.

"Six or seven. Maybe he was the seventh. Three were burned dead and three fell off the edge of a waterfall when the beams came down. And drowned. He was part-burned and fell over too."

"No. Hank lies."

"Well, he survived."

"And he tells that goddamned tale, maybe four thousand times. His mind's blown. Some of 'em say he wasn't anywhere but in the truck. But anyway, he's crazy about hurt guys. I was in the hospital. Almost never got rid of him. He'll find your ass if you're injured, blow in your ear all day."

"Yeah," says the married man.

"Sad," says Polly. "Six dead." She reflects soberly.

Hank has found her and doesn't seem to understand at all. He drills her with a level searching lunatic study. Polly looks at him and shifts. She's frightened.

"Polly," says the married man. He puts his hand over hers. She jumps.

Hank can't stand it any longer.

"Seven Dead in City Lights Calamity!" he announces, wide-eyed and raising his twisted hand.

Polly is horrified.

"I don't like you." It comes out despite herself.

Hank turns away.

"He's harmless," says the married man.

"I don't like that man. He better stay away."

"Some of 'em," says the careless worker, "they say he *loves* injuries, deaths, trouble. Waiting for another big thing. Might . . . be bringing it on."

"Cram it, Rodney," she says.

The married man is hurt by another trespass of her tongue.

The man with the handsome brown fingers is in front of his mirror now and we see him. His face is of a Eurasian cast. He wears rimless spectacles, and there is a far-off crystalline glint in his brown eyes. He is rather scruffy, has forgotten his appearance, and now rubs the small mask of whiskers on his chin and cheeks. His hair is black, tossed at odd angles like a stack of hay. He removes his glasses, opens his fatigued, solemn eyes to the stretching point, rubs the dark circles underneath. His mission is less anxious now. He lifts a slight smile. It has been unnatural of him to smile lately. He explores the smile, lifting the corners of his mouth with more adventure, stops just short of a loony diameter.

The long privacy, the meditation, the ardent expectation—all of these are seen in his expression as he uses the razor, lathering himself with a bar of hotel soap. Weariness falls from him as he washes the whiskers away. The face is the color of creamed coffee. Its nature is strong but ascetic. He removes his soiled blue shirt, splashes water on his chest. His body has been exercised: he's in fine enough shape. We see that he is a man of deeds, a man set on a journey of some moment. There is a positive physicality to him. Yet some of his movements are awkward. He does not seem quite trained for the regular day. He blinks quite often. And, when, finishing his stand-up toilet, he lights a cigarette, it is clumsy. The process seems a bit foreign to him. He overlights, holding the match too long; the cigarette is bent a little; the puffs after intake are rapid, like those of a child on his first few attempts.

He goes back to his table and straightens the pages next to his dictionary. There are fresh stacked and addressed envelopes. He spies the top sheet of paper and holds it, fixing the glasses back on his nose. The word *reluctance* is written in a column several times. He has some difficulty pronouncing it aloud.

"*Ree* . . . Luck . . . Tense. No. Re . . . Luck . . . Tunce. *Uhnss*." Satisfied. Again.

The cigarette has burned down to his fingers. It scores him. He drops the butt and sucks his fingers. The pain, which must be considerable, does not impress him too much.

There is a long scar on his right underforearm,

perhaps from a knife. And there is a white crescent scar on his chin. One of his front teeth is chipped. But he seems too fastidious to be a roadhouse warrior.

He goes to his window with the binoculars. The view downward is the edge of metropolitan Seattle, the beginning of small shops and residences. He can see, almost directly down, the kiosk of the old hippie and witness blind Little Willy in his tall silver cowboy hat. It is a pleasant, neighborly urban Seattle he sees, a brisk and friendly area.

He spies three women walking together past the kiosk, Little Willy celebrating them, one of them stopping to throw some change from her jeans pocket into his cigar box. The three women wear jeans and colored flannel shirts, sneakers, and buckskin flats. The binocular's view remains on them and their passage up the street. Their hips swing loosely, their strides confident, graceful with surfaces; their arms are free, gesticulating with an abundant, open strife in their conversation. They might be girls from the shipyards, many lady things to share on their day off. The man smiles.

"Women . . . doing large things. Outdoor women. Breathing big air women."

This pleases him very much.

He goes to get his corduroy jacket from the back of his chair. He gathers the brown envelopes. He goes into the bathroom and views himself again, straightens the tucked collar of his jacket, neatens the collar of his fresh green shirt.

"I think we will . . . have a *hamburger*," he says, approving of himself. "Maybe *two* juicy hamburgers."

He leaves the bathroom and goes to the door but returns to the mirror.

"And two steaming cups of rich *coffee*." He winks —gives a slow awkward wink.

Then he disappears.

Vision lowers on a huge lift crane at the shipyard. It is a staggering ingenious strength, even a cumbersome grace, at the docks. Men are around, but they are dwarfed by the monster, made irrelevant. This behemoth moves with an amazing precision, plucking now a giant carburetor from the wharf ground and swinging it to the deck, then down to the hold of the unfinished ship. Beethoven comes on with a power symphony and we hear grand strains of German pomposity.

In the pilot's cabin is the black woman with the levers. She wears a metal helmet and eye protectors— vast goggles in which her eyes swim over the dull light of the sodden day. They are welding all around her. There are smoking pots, debris, heaps of steel. Construction is pressing on, but it is as if a tank attack has passed through and we witness the wreckage of victory, a slain fantastic fortress spilling around us. The crane draws off the hold of the ship, heaving empty after settling its load.

However, there is something odd in the pilot's cabin—narrowing in through the wharf debris, narrowing in to the swift certain hands of the black woman, chocolate-colored sinews of her hands drawing tight, veins apparent, we view her face, and now we see the little flinches of the eyes, quick minuscule drops of sweat that betray a woman possessed by a steady terror. But she has a stern professional mien and control. Nothing is amiss with the crane. Yet it is a confounding schizophrenic vision to witness its operation in the hands of a haunted woman.

Then, standing among the hard hats, entirely out of place and being reprimanded by a few workers, Lou appears. He is pathetically thin, an old Bogart fedora on him. The paint and the heedlessness are gone, but this specter is sick. His suit is of an unseasonal light weave, wrinkled, and he wears a tie over an orange shirt, a bad mixed-plaid greenish one. He is eminently lonely, staring at the black woman in the pilot house. Workers around him give way, recognizing something grievous, pathological. He doesn't walk right when he begins walking. He walks, bends at the knees—will he fall?—and clutches at a crate. Even the sea gulls flee from him. He fumbles for a cigarette and breaks half of it, starting a messy fire around his lips. He has more sick desperation than confidence, though he is trying for something robust in his walk.

The black woman sees him. Everything stops. We can't see the change behind the goggles, but her face snaps to. She steps down. Workers in the blurred yard are watching. Lou augments everything they've ever thought about "niggers" at their worst, and they are happily gouging in with their comments.

"Maureen," says Lou, panting.

"Lou?" She's embarrassed, chagrined.

"I need money, Maureen."

"Ah, Lou." She removes the glove from her left hand. "You don't need nothing but a hospital."

She glances, without the goggles now, anxiously around the wharf yard, perhaps fearing the foreman.

"Money, Maureen. Sis."

"I'll give you my insurance card," the black woman says. "You covered. You got to go to the hospital, then we'll talk about money."

She reaches for the wallet in her jeans.

"Take the card, go—"

"I ain't the sick!" He begins crying and trembling. "Money!" He collapses on her.

She puts the card in his hand, with a five dollar bill.

Now all is quiet except for the yakking of the gulls. The workers are still, transfixed, paralyzed in forms of attentive statuary. It is phenomenal what interest the black woman and her brother have drawn. No gesture seems possible.

The man with the white bulldog is at the kiosk of the old hippie, buying a magazine, which he opens with a public sneer. Little Willy, blind with the harmonica, wearing the tall silver hat, ends up a riff badly.

"Cocksucker!" the little brat says, cuffing the large harmonica with his tiny paw. He edges into the rear of the dog and it turns around to face him, smushed curiosity on its face.

Little Willy smiles, kneels to pat the dog. He finds its face with one hand, takes his cowboy hat off with the other. The child's hair is greasy and long. He puts the giant hat over the dog's face.

The man at the end of the leash is pulled and notices now.

He looks guardedly around and then takes a fierce swipe at the boy, really smacks him across the head, and the child reels off a stumbling two yards, dropping his harmonica. The man steps over and crushes the harmonica with the heel of his oxbloods.

"You were made for the gashouse, little friend!" says the bulldog man. His oxblood shoes comes down on the cigar box on the walk and breaks out its coins.

The old hippie is trying to unlock his counter and swing out for some assistance.

"Buddy! Mister!" he shouts, a mild groover outraged.

"Okay, okay," pants the man, calming, pacifying the hippie with supplicant hands. "Just don't forget. It wasn't meant for all sorts of things to go on. Just *any*-thing. Okay?"

The man we saw in the hotel room is still pleased. He is finishing a hamburger and holds his hand up for another. The burger must be especially tasty. The coffee he drinks seems extraordinarily good, too. The fellow is neat and healthy and rather scholarly in his rimless glasses; neat, that is, except for a missed tuck of his green shirt. One collar hangs out, the other under his coat. Something about him, like incomplete dressing practice when young, some simple skill not yet accomplished, marks his manner. With the café life quiet around him, there is an almost childish satisfaction with the food and drink. He turns to a couple on the two stools to his left.

"Good burgers!" he advocates, giving a wink.
"Uh? Yeh."

Then he becomes suddenly very meditative. His expression has the small beginning of a smile, a careful postured study, quick.

Four women, Angel, Polly, Maureen, and someone as yet unseen, Cornelia the doctor—a woman with a cheerful but drawn, baggy-eyed face in her late thirties—walk in together. There has been some meeting. They have mimeographed literature in their hands. Cornelia asks the waitress for the direction to the trash barrel, and she and then Polly ball their leaflets up and toss them over the counter.

"And give me a beer. Pronto," says Cornelia.

"Nothing good ever happened anyway at any meeting I ever went to," says Polly.

They all get comfortable in the far booth at the window. The waitress comes over and they order beer and coffee.

The table is quiet. There is some interlude of concern from the others as Cornelia orders another beer. "So why do we go to the meetings at all if everything's peachy?" asks Cornelia.

They all give this matter a bit of study.

"Well, it's not all peachy. Some things have got to be done. Like the letters, those brown damned letters. What gives some son of a bitch the freedom to write such letters to us? He can be found and prosecuted and buried is what. Get rid of that son of a bitch out there who's always murking it up," says Polly.

"Ah. It's just a religious nut. Shouldn't bother you," says Angel.

"I *liked* the 'appointment with something *large*'

part. It's kind of zesty. I *hope* so. Old Charlie's the last of the functional three-inchers. Somebody's got a crush on all us wonderful girls," says Cornelia.

"Well, I'm *not* religious. And I'm not available for some sickie's crush, and I should have the right not to be," speaks Polly, loudly. "I don't want any appointments. I don't want anything queer."

Cornelia has grown solemn.

"But there's *always* an appointment, isn't there? There's always," she says.

They all reflect unpleasantly, ruminatively about this.

The man of the hotel room stares straight ahead. The waitress asks him, is ignored.

"I said do you want more coffee. Hey. Dreamer!"

"That's good. Oh, that's good. That's perfect."

Ruth, blond Ruth of the hidden fits, is talking, rather businesslike. There is something masculine and reasonable about her voice, a stern divulgence, as if she were calling altitudes to control personnel. And that is all right, seeing her face only. She might be watching someone place a picture on the wall. Her eyes are far-off, her voice accurate, measured.

"That's about as good as can be. I can't believe it's going so well. This is flying. This is really, really flying."

Here, with a fast scan shot of the City Lights Powerhouse, we see immense cables of various colors, the dynamo whirring, where Polly Buck and the boys do their business; out to poles, crossed thick wires spraying art under a gray sky running to calm residential streets, back to the waterfall of the Cascades.

Cables sing, citizens! Mister Kilowatt is dashing on his errands, to wires entering Ruth's splendid little hideaway apartment to wires coming out of her wall under her bed.

"It's breaking down now. It's getting milky."

There is a pleased dreamy gaze in her eyes. Then she shuts her eyes. The lashes are long and voluptuous.

Her hand reaches, clutching, down the side of the bed. Her hand is a dear sensual sight, with her sterling jadestone ring, opalescent pink nail polish. But the fingers find a wire under the bed, clutch it. There is something weighty to it. The fingers then clasp on the wire and pull it. There is something.

"Don't stop . . . don't stop."

She pulls up a cassette recorder, reels running. Her shoulders are bare, we see now. The pillow behind her is mauve, lacy at the edges. Her blond hair spreads and halos her head. She looks at the turning reels.

"Thank you, everybody. That's all," she says. She is holding her anger.

"Huh?" a male voice comes from below her. Ian is unseen, but his pedagogical voice clears itself, states, "What's the problem?"

"You crooked, prissy . . . professor."

"Huh?"

She holds up the little machine by the wire.

"How long have I been on the air, Professor?"

. . .

Honey Jefferson is at the typewriter, just off the dispatcher's office where Angel St. James is calling and listening.

Honey is tiny. Her decor is an apotheosis of the tiny—lilac-and-lime dress on, fragile jewelry at her wrist and ears. Her desk is crowded but blamelessly neat. Neatness is a small tyrant at this desk.

Honey allows herself a short daydream, lip-speaks some lines.

"Some day, some day," she hums, transfixed to her dream. But very fast she's back to order.

"Some day what?" Angel has stopped beside her desk.

"Oh just some day."

"Honey. You're so cute. You're so tiny." This comes sincerely from Angel, a happy advocate. She looks maternally at the cunning little lady.

"But there's not that much to me," says Honey. She seems not too saddened by this dreadful truth.

"Sure there is. I bet you dream big. You might be a girl Napoléon."

"Oh, sure. Like Napoléon and Juliet. But I'm so tiny. I'm too tiny. I'm a Tinkerbell. It's what Doodad calls me. You can't barely see me. Look at my little hands." They are indeed doll's hands.

Angel looks at her own hands. They're white and nice but seasoned with lines.

"The both of us together, Doodad and me, we might be something. He's the sweetest big thing. And strong. He goes to school at night."

Angel is not sold on the prospect of Doodad. Her eyes wrinkle up to refuse it.

"You're talking under my head. Think of what you could've had by now."

"Angel, you forget I'm so *little*. I can't lift all those, can't operate all those—"

"I told you. There's lots of field jobs where it's better to be little. Small people do a lot. Don't you think the Japanese have the handle on a hell of a lot of things? Like almost the whole *place?*"

"Well, I'm American," Honey states positively.

Angel nods. "What does *that* mean? You're still way under my head."

"Well, I don't use jibber talk or eat fried leaves, either. I like the man to drive. Who said the man's not always supposed to drive? Who made up all these new Japanese rules?" Her voice is light but feisty.

Angel is straightening this with her brows, attempting it.

"They made up the term *pink collar* just for you, Honey."

"Communism has nothing to do with it, either. Everybody wasn't made to break the pattern like you. We can't all be rough and sweaty and . . . think. I don't mean you—"

"That's okay. Go ahead and let Doodad get everything for you. You could probably tiny him around the rest of your life. I'll bet you'll be the cutest little hornet."

"I was sitting here doing my job."

"Honey, for five years you've just been sitting there being highly visible. You're just a little gem." Angel neither smiles nor frowns.

"Thanks," says Honey. She blushes.

. . .

Cornelia, the doctor, is curing her hangover. There is a half-eaten chili dog on her littered desk, at which she winces. She is rumpled in her white smock, having slept in her office the night previous. She fetches out a bottle, gets a beaker, produces two eggs from her desk drawer, breaks them, pours whiskey over the eggs, and downs the mixture with three gagging spaced gulps. The immediate relief afforded by the whiskey is apparent with her closed eyes. Her face comes to life as if out of a cold wash. She lights a Camel. There is a knock at the door, but Cornelia says, "Not yet."

She douses a good amount in the beaker again, downs that.

"Not please yet, O heavenly hosts."

She pulls out the day's charts and looks at them.

She gets out a yellow pad, begins writing.

"Hello. This is going to hurt. Good-bye."

She continues marking.

"Hello. Better do your Christmas shopping real early. Good-bye."

She continues, takes a sip from the film in the beaker.

"Hello. I never had an orgasm either. Good-bye."

She quits marking.

"Hello, new patient. Meet an ageing pregnant drunk."

Cornelia drops the pad. She is caught by a sober meditation, touches her miscombed hair.

. . .

Ladies and Gentlemen,

Polly Buck and Larry Lynn are strolling in a run-down damp park of Seattle, the wind up, toying with the loose fetching hair of Polly. Polly is more winsome, nymphlike here than we have seen her, victim of her gloomy thoughts and of the wind. Nature lies around them soggy and twisted, flattening the sounds of their footsteps, muffling them.

The man with the bulldog watches from a stand of trees. He observes Larry Lynn place her arm on Polly Buck and hug her.

In Puget Sound—our eye is on the dark, rolling, forbidding water. Comes an eruption of foam, bubbles under the waves, then the appearance of a conning tower, higher, higher, astonishing. It is an atomic submarine, a staggering long cigar of black. The hatch door opens. Far away and dull shine the lights of Seattle. A captain's hat rises and the man himself steps out. He is alone. There is light from below through the hatchdoor.

He stares at the shore. This man is something haggard.

Now we see the rolled sleeves and bitten nails of a hard-pressed woman. It is Irene Zolta, nervous and fever eyed. Perhaps a cigarette has never been smoked this viciously. Smoke rolls out and she's outraged, as if surprised. She coughs. Her nose is ahead, busy as a hound's. She's got a sheaf of announcements in her hand, a grave purpose. There seems to be some nasty impediment to all her moves. Out of the way, things! She is near the dispatcher's office of City Lights. She casts around, spies tiny Honey Jefferson.

This is activism, citizens, of the roving hyena sort. Little Honey seems to be the perfect dead bait. Pretty shortly Irene is upon her, brandishing her leaflets, half-prepared already to spit in disgust. It is near closing time and a rangy basketball kind of guy hangs visible near the exit, waiting on tiny Honey to finish her chores.

Today Honey is dressed all pink and white.

It is Angel and Fritz Walls, nighttime in his living room. The television is beaming away with a multiple car wreck. Beer is being drunk. Legs are on the coffee table. There are no magazines and the picture on the wall is an item of mass-reproducible desert flats, cow skull in the foreground.

Walls wears orange sneakers. He might be a couple of years younger than Angel, but he seems to have achieved a stable age years ago, from which he cannot wander far. His face has an ashen stubble, and he peers unwondering although mesmerized at the television.

When the teevee movie ends, it seems to bring down the night, last act. Which is that Fritz and Angel rise as if in sync and file to his bedroom, Fritz shutting off the lamp.

Not a word is said.

There are some mechanical sounds of the necessaries in the boudoir. But no words or cries are heard.

We have an outview of two dark houses, Angel's and Fritz's. How convenient.

Sighs are not heard. Even minor remarks are not heard.

The clammy palm of Seattle supports the hedges, the patios, the automobiles.

Walls's humor is revealed on the bumper sticker of his dim Plymouth: "Warning—I Brake for Penguins."

This is not Seattle. We look upon the desert and high rock struts of black mountains, a violent blue sky. Then we close in on Miramar Naval Air Station, San Diego. F-5s, F-8s, F-4s, Ov-10s, and F-14s sit around the tarmac and in the immense hangars.

There is an F-14, the Tomcat, on approach. It is a beautiful double-tailed demon, seeking the floor.

In the cockpit is Ruth, forward as pilot, another as radarman in the behind seat. There is little sound inside. Ruth's face is strained. She looks into the sky. She has sweat and tremors about the lips. The girl is scared.

Something is refractory.

The plane faults the approach, levels, rises.

The radarman behind is smirking, rather enjoying this.

"You going to put this thing down?"

Ruth says nothing. She seems to have forgotten how to land and nods her head over an implausible loss.

The radarman is sternly noting this. He has plans on the ground and is thoroughly miffed.

. . .

Ladies and Gentlemen,

Polly Buck. A curious pass. She stands in front of a large, sprawling house with a fountain outside. It is a suburban dream. Her eyes are sad but determined. She goes up to the door.

The next we see of her, she's sitting in a very masculine den room. The magazines on a mahogany block table are exotic geographical reviews with startling expensive photos. The appointments are leather, antlers, shields, tribal instruments and weapons such as some white people gather about for rare karma. She sits on a zebra couch.

Her hair is parted in the middle—winsome, maidenlike. A teacup is in front of her on the table. A flower is at her ear, and it poses agreeably against her light freckles.

"Maybe it's bad," she said. "But I had to . . . I'm still leaving blood from us . . . I can't love . . . something is going to happen . . . I get these notes. I know you didn't send the notes."

"No. Sometimes, Polly, in order to grow, we have to learn to forget, to let go."

We have not seen the man. His voice is earnest, rather clinical.

The teacup trembles in Polly's hand.

Cornelia and Lou, Maureen's junkie brother, share the same room on the fourth floor of a great Seattle hospital. Cornelia lies quietly in the bed near the window. It's late dusk, a purplish gray outside.

Lou is shifting about, mumbling in his bed nearest the door. The beds are separated by a folding beige partition. Lou is shaking the bed and making some racket.

"For God's sake, keep it down," says Cornelia.

"I ain't no woman. They put me in here with a woman!" Lou shouts.

Hospital Hank, from the bar episode, appears at the door. He peers in at Lou trembling on the bed. He flirts with the light switch, then turns on the lights of the room.

Ladies and Gentlemen,

Polly Buck, in her apartment, looks at a newly arrived note on brown paper:

So close. My ears are dead but I am happy my eyes are not. You are the woman. No person else. You shall. You shall.
                                        Sweed Truitt

She folds the note and pushes it sternly back into the envelope, which she also folds and pushes into the back pocket of her trousers, newly bought for the visit of her folks from Idaho, who are in the house now, Mother and Father Buck, talking cautiously to the great form of Larry Lynn. Larry Lynn has gained poise since learning she has no cancer, and she looks pregnant in her dark brown pants suit and brass necklace.

Polly's father, just slightly backward as Idaho people go, comes out into the foyer where Polly is. He's a little charged with the Johnnie Walker Red behind him on the coffee table, but one knows he's a good kind by his dazzling blue eyes and kind mouth, the lips pursing as he prepares to understand his strange grown daughter.

"I frankly don't mind her at all. Polly. It's all right if you . . . you two . . . the two of you . . . are different and have found your nest. Maybe to rise in our cities as a woman there is a difference . . . a great difference. You rise high enough, you have to change."

"What you think is I'm a lesbian. I'm not. She's only my fat friend," says Polly Buck.

Mr. Buck is startled, but then he's very happy. "You're not?"

He starts giggling, even slaps his thigh. This father from Idaho is delighted.

Polly's mother is in the background, talking to Larry Lynn. The two of them are getting on well, now the man's not there. Polly and Mr. Buck regard them. They have quiet smiles on their faces. Polly looks like the lovely gladiator that she is.

Ladies and Gentlemen,

Jimi Hendrix plays the guitar, a very young lad with a cheap guitar plugged into a flaky amplifier.

Polly Buck climbs a light pole to his amateurish licks. There is a great lightning storm and Polly is working with her big screwdriver. The ocean is heaving up and the lightning is flashing against her. A piece of lightning hits her helmet and her helmet flies off. She keeps working, she keeps working, she keeps working.

In the harbor her boat is wrecked. It heaves up and crashes on the dock.